A Wind of

Change

A Shade of Vampire, Book 17

Bella Forrest

Also by Bella Forrest:

A SHADE OF VAMPIRE SERIES:

Derek & Sofia's story:

A Shade of Vampire (Book 1)
A Shade of Blood (Book 2)
A Castle of Sand (Book 3)
A Shadow of Light (Book 4)
A Blaze of Sun (Book 5)
A Gate of Night (Book 6)
A Break of Day (Book 7)

Rose & Caleb's story:

A Shade of Novak (Book 8)
A Bond of Blood (Book 9)
A Spell of Time (Book 10)
A Chase of Prey (Book 11)
A Shade of Doubt (Book 12)
A Turn of Tides (Book 13)
A Dawn of Strength (Book 14)
A Fall of Secrets (Book 15)
An End of Night (Book 16)

The Shade lives on...

A Wind of Change (Book 17)

A SHADE OF KIEV TRILOGY:

A Shade of Kiev 1
A Shade of Kiev 2
A Shade of Kiev 3

BEAUTIFUL MONSTER DUOLOGY:

Beautiful Monster 1
Beautiful Monster 2

For an updated list of Bella's books,
please visit www.bellaforrest.net

Contents

PROLOGUE: BEN

I ran the entire circumference of the boundary surrounding The Oasis. There was no way out. The brand on my upper right arm burned more than ever. It felt like my skin was on fire.

There was no point trying to break through any longer. I wasn't going to escape. Not now and not like this.

I had to return before someone noticed me up here. I hoped that Marilyn had been too drunk to remember what had happened once she woke from sleep.

I hurried back across the sand toward The Oasis. I was within one mile of it when I spotted something north of the coven's entrance. A stable, filled with camels. There must've been at least fifty of them. I wasn't sure why they were there, because Jeramiah and his people seemed to have no shortage of human blood in their cellars. I couldn't imagine why they needed camel blood too. Tearing my eyes away from the stable, I raced back toward the trapdoor leading down toward the atrium.

Before descending the staircase, I poked my head down through the hole in the ground as far as I could and looked around, listening for any sign of someone having woken up nearby. I could hear heavy breathing, and the occasional snore. As far as I could tell, everyone was in bed. I climbed down the stairs and closed the trapdoor above me as quietly as I could.

Almost as soon as my feet touched the floor, the burning in my arm stopped. I thought I might have been hallucinating at first. Then I wondered whether the hot air outside had aggravated it. It was bizarre. I could still feel it prickling slightly, but the pain was nowhere near as agonizing as before.

I lowered the sheet filled with sacks of blood that I had flung over my shoulder, and proceeded to take off layer after layer of shirts I had piled on. I didn't want to be caught looking like I had just tried to escape.

I stopped peeling off the layers as I reached the last one. Bunching up the clothing under my left arm, I picked up the bundle of blood and tucked that under my right arm. Although I looked less suspicious without so many shirts, if I bumped into a vampire they would smell the blood. I had to move quickly before anyone started waking up.

I took the elevator down to my level and sprinted along the winding veranda toward my apartment door. It was wide open. I stepped inside and locked the door. Heading straight to my bedroom, I expected the worst—that Marilyn was still in here. But she wasn't. I searched the rest of the apartment just to be sure. She had gone. Perhaps she had returned to Jeramiah, or taken up my suggestion to find some other apartment to sleep in.

Heading for my bathroom, I removed the two pairs

of pants I had layered on, then removed my shirt. I stared at myself in the mirror. My breath hitched at the sight of the tattoo. Previously pitch black, now it was tinged red. The skin around it was glowing, like an ember dying down after a fire. This was no ordinary tattoo. It clearly had some kind of magical power. Perhaps one of the witches residing here had etched it into me…

I grabbed a towel from the railing and wet it with cold water, then dabbed it over the tattoo. I held it there for about ten minutes before letting it go. The prickling was practically nonexistent by now, and the glowing of the tattoo seemed to have died down.

Then I stepped into the shower and turned on the cold water, calming the rest of my body after being exposed to the sweltering heat outside. Once I had finished showering, I dried myself, pulled on a clean pair of pants and another shirt, then returned to my bedroom. I walked to the bed and sat down on the edge of it.

What now?

I rested my head in my hands, closing my eyes and

trying to plan my next step.

I had to escape. That much hadn't changed.

Jeramiah had told me about the boundary—and warned me not to go near it. He'd told me the story of the vampire who used to live in this very apartment, who had gotten drunk and ventured outside, only to be killed by the hunters who patrolled this area closely.

I had assumed that I would have the freedom to step outside, just as that vampire had, however dangerous it was. I could only guess that the witches had set up this barrier spell and hadn't yet granted me permission to come in and out as I pleased.

My first step became clear to me. I had to gain these people's trust, by whatever means necessary.

And that meant only one thing: I had to seek out Jeramiah. He was the clear leader of this place. If I gained his trust, everything else would follow.

I stood up and paced around the room. Now that I knew Jeramiah was the bastard child of my uncle, conceived before Lucas turned into a vampire, just the thought of looking him in the eye felt so awkward. Although I guessed that he didn't know I was Derek

Novak's son, and indeed believed that my name was Joseph Brunson, there was no way I could be completely sure.

Still, it wasn't like I had any other choice.

I picked up the sheet wrapped with blood sacks from the floor and took it into the kitchen. Rolling it out on the table, I picked up the sacks and replaced them in the fridge—except for one, which I poured into a glass and drank. I needed some blood in my system for what was ahead of me.

Then I left my apartment. As I looked around my level, people were beginning to wake up and step out of their apartments. There was still no sign of Marilyn.

"Joseph," a male voice called behind me.

I turned around to find myself face to face with one of the vampires from the crowd the night before, when Jeramiah had introduced me to everybody. He had short hair and a nose that was disproportionately large.

"Good morning... Or good day, whatever time it is," he said, grinning. "I'm Lloyd."

"Good day," I said, even though this day felt like it couldn't have been any worse.

"You look a bit lost," he said.

"Not lost," I replied. "Have you seen Jeramiah around?"

He gestured toward the gardens down below in the center of the atrium. Walking over to the railing, he pointed down toward the lily pond—where Lucas Novak's memorial stone lay. About ten feet away from the edge of the water, sitting cross-legged and shirtless on the lawn, was Jeramiah. His hair was bunched up in a bun on top of his head and he sat motionless, his eyes closed. He had an expression of serenity on his face.

"He's meditating," Lloyd said.

Meditating?

"He does it every morning. He finds it strengthens the mind. Before he got turned, he spent time in India with a bunch of yogis. Learned about mind and self-control… Whatever," he said, turning back to me. "Anyway, good to have you here, Joseph. I live just five doors down from you, if you need help with anything…"

"Thanks," I said.

He turned and walked away.

I fixed my eyes back down on the vampire sitting in the center of the lawn. He began inhaling deeply, his back straight. I remained watching him for the next twenty minutes until he finally opened his eyes and stood up. He moved closer to the lily pond. Before he could disappear, I took the opportunity to join him downstairs. He sensed me approaching, and turned around to face me.

"Ah, Joseph. How did you sleep?"

"Well," I said coolly. I stood next to him by the water's edge.

"Good," he said. "Good."

There was no point in bringing up the tattoo on my arm. He was showing no signs of offering an explanation about it, so I was not going to mention it. It would only be counterproductive. And what would I say anyway? Obviously one of them here had done it, it was just a question of who. A minor detail. The fact was that the mark had been etched into me at Jeramiah's order.

Still, I found it odd that he felt no need to offer me the slightest bit of explanation for it.

"I'm sorry I had to leave early last night," I said, watching his reaction carefully. "As I said, I wasn't feeling well."

"That's all right. We understood. I guess all of this"—he gestured around the atrium—"is a lot to take in for a newcomer. The desert air can also have a strange effect on people who aren't used to it. Especially in these parts…"

"I also realized that I have not thanked you properly," I continued. "First of all for saving me from those hunters back in Chile, and then offering me refuge here."

"That's quite all right," he said, looking me over thoughtfully. "I like you already, Joseph. I'm sure you'll prove to be a valuable addition to our coven and won't let us down." He paused, fixing his eyes back on the lily pond. "I'm generally an easy person to get along with in any case." His gaze shot back to me. "Just don't ever lie to me. Because I don't tolerate liars."

I looked back at him unflinchingly, though inside I was taken aback. It made me wonder whether he suspected I wasn't being truthful about my identity.

But his appearance resumed its previous zen state and he looked back at the blue lilies.

"As I said before," he continued, "I'm sure that you will like it here. It might take some getting used to, but once you do, you will never want to leave."

"I'm sure I won't," I said.

Marilyn had better have forgotten what she witnessed last night.

"I realize that I still know very little about this place," I said, looking around the magnificent atrium. "I would like to know more. You mentioned how you found it and rebuilt it into what it is today, but I'm curious about how you manage the logistics. Like, how do you get humans down here?"

Jeramiah gestured to a wooden bench by the side of the pond and we both sat down.

"Much the same as any vampire procures human blood. We go out on hunts, usually catching a large number of humans at the same time, and then one of our six witches transports us back. We rarely step directly out of the boundary of The Oasis—we travel places by magic in order to avoid the hunters stationed outside."

"I see. And you keep all the humans down in the basement, don't you?" I asked, recalling my own brief venture down there.

"Yes. We store humans down there but also some half-blood slaves. Many of the half-bloods live with vampires in apartments—mostly in servant quarters—but others remain downstairs."

"And how many vampires are there here? How many half-bloods?"

"Three hundred and twenty vampires, and one hundred and sixty half-bloods," he replied without hesitation.

I raised a brow. "You like to keep the ratio precise."

"Yes."

He didn't offer any further explanation as to why that was, and I didn't ask.

"And how many humans do you typically keep down there?" I asked, gesturing to the ground.

"It varies."

"And why is it their blood tastes so good? It's the best I've tasted."

A broad smile formed on his lips. "We keep our humans exceptionally well. We feed them a healthy diet and keep them free from diseases. Of course, it has an effect on the blood."

"I see." That hadn't been the answer I had been expecting, but I supposed it made sense. "And you manage this place alone?"

"Amaya, Michael and I do most of the managing. But since everyone around here is an adult—although some can certainly act like children—keeping things in order isn't too taxing. We've been living here long enough to work out systems. Everyone knows their role in helping out and keeping everything running smoothly."

This was the opening I was looking for all along.

"Speaking of helping," I said, "I feel indebted. Is there something I can do to play my part?"

"Yes," he said. "You won't be useful in hunting any humans right now, being newly turned—but there are certainly other things you can help with."

I tried to hide my frustration. "I feel more confident in my ability to control myself around humans. But you're right, it's perhaps still too early."

I should have laughed at the understatement. I still had zero confidence around humans. It was a wonder that I had managed to keep myself from attacking any humans when I had gone down to the basement. The fact that they were locked in secure rooms had helped. Still, even then I'd been scared that I would break inside and steal one. It was a good thing that my venture downstairs had only been quick.

"So if you're ready to start helping, come with me," he said. He began walking away from the pond and the gardens and led me toward one of the rooms on the atrium's ground level. The door was unlocked and he pushed it open. Stepping inside after him, I found myself in a large dim storage chamber. It smelled of… some kind of animal. Reins and harnesses hung from the ceiling. Jeramiah headed straight for a corner where there was a pile of metal buckets covered with lids. He picked up six by the handle, balancing three in each hand, and gave them to me.

"Above ground we have a stable of camels. Go and fill these buckets with milk."

I stared at him, wondering if this was some kind of joke.

"Milk? What do you use milk for?"

"The humans," he said. "I told you we make sure that they get proper nutrition."

I stared down at the buckets. "Sure," I replied, although I was anything but.

We exited the room and Jeramiah and I parted. I made my way up to the top level in one of the elevators. I was still thinking about how strange this request was even as I climbed through the trapdoor and stepped out once again into the hot desert. Even though the sun wasn't shining directly upon me, due to the witches' spell of night around this area, I could still feel the heat now that I was outside of the cool atmosphere of The Oasis.

They needed milk for the humans. I wondered why the witches didn't just provide it by magic. I didn't understand why they bothered with mundane labor like this.

Milking camels. I let the thought sink in. I sure hadn't thought this would be what Jeramiah would ask of me.

A part of me had been expecting him to ask me to half-turn one of the humans. I was relieved he hadn't, of course. I would have ended up murdering them. The only reason I'd been able to control myself around Tobias was because he was sick. I doubted I would be able to refrain from devouring a healthy human, especially such a healthy human as the ones they kept down in the basement. Their blood truly tasted divine.

I headed for the stable I had spotted earlier, the buckets clinking at my sides.

Milkman Benjamin.

I imagined my sister would get a kick out of that image.

My sister. The thought that I was a threat to even her now made my gut clench.

I have to figure out why I've turned into this monster.

But first, I need to escape this place.

I arrived at the stable, entered it, and walked along the aisles of slobbering camels until I spotted Michael, bending down in one corner over a bucket milking a particularly stout camel. After learning from Jeramiah that he was one of the managers of The Oasis, I was surprised to see him doing such a menial job.

He didn't even look up as I approached, although he had obviously sensed me.

He had been nothing but frosty with me since the time I had first met him with Jeramiah in Chile. I had no interest in trying to spark up a conversation so I ignored him too. Though it would have been useful to get at least some direction as to how to milk a camel.

Walking further down the aisles, I picked a camel who seemed to have a particularly swollen udder and placed the bucket on the floor. As I motioned to touch her, she jerked backward and began grunting and kicking wildly. One of her heavy feet narrowly missed my right foot.

I stood up and placed both hands firmly on her back, trying to calm her.

"It's okay, girl."

Believe me, I'm as uncomfortable about this as you are.

My body expelled animal blood like it was poison anyway. Any fear this creature had of me was unfounded. I approached her head and stroked her long neck. That seemed to calm her down gradually and she stopped struggling. I bent down and started squeezing the milk from her teats. This time she remained still for me—well, still enough for milk to start squirting into the first bucket.

Once she seemed to be growing uncomfortable again, I moved on to the next camel. Then the next. And the next. Until all six buckets were filled up with the frothy white liquid. Wiping my sticky hands against a towel hanging on a hook, I looked around the stable for Michael. I couldn't see him. He appeared to have finished his work and returned to The Oasis.

I was glad that the buckets came with lids. If they hadn't, I would've spilled a lot of the milk on my journey back. The lids were tight, but balancing six heavy buckets of milk was a challenge even for a vampire. My palms were only so big. Still, going slowly and taking care not to slosh the milk too much, I reached the entrance of The Oasis and descended the staircase.

I took the elevator down to the ground floor. Looking out across the gardens, I spotted Jeramiah by the lily pond again. He was talking with a female vampire I didn't know the name of but had seen the night before.

"Jeramiah. What do you want me to do with these?" I asked, nodding to the buckets.

"Ah," he said, looking pleased as he eyed the large buckets. He left his female companion and approached me. Taking three buckets from me, he led me back toward the bottom terrace. We headed straight for the room that led down to the prison. We both took the buckets inside, and as we reached the door at the back of the room, I noticed that the lock had been replaced. It looked much stronger and sturdier. When Jeramiah drew out a key from his pocket, I could see from the way that it was molded that this was a much more complicated lock—much more difficult to pick than the one I'd managed to crack.

I wondered whether they'd found out that someone had been down there—and that the intruder had been me.

Or perhaps it was a coincidence.

A very odd coincidence.

As he opened the door and stepped inside with three buckets, I motioned to follow him. Planting his buckets on the floor, he swiveled back around and held up a hand, blocking the entrance.

"I'll take these. Thanks."

He took the three buckets from me, placed them on the ground next to the others, and then closed the door behind him. There was a sharp click as the door locked.

A delicious aroma wafted into my nostrils from down below. I could appreciate the smell even as a vampire. Someone was cooking something exotic in the basement. It must have been for the humans. I was curious as to who exactly was doing the cooking and where. I had not noticed any kitchens. Then again, I'd only explored a small part of the maze that was their prison system. I actually had no idea how big it was. For all I knew, it could be spread out over several levels underground.

I decided to wait for Jeramiah to return. He did about five minutes later, locking the door behind him and slipping the key into the right pocket of his pants.

He flashed me a smile. "That can be a morning duty

for you from now on. Six buckets of camel milk. I have to think what else you can help with around here. I'm going to discuss it with Amaya and Michael."

"I was surprised to see Michael up there milking," I said.

"Yes. Well, we don't like too much hierarchy among us. Even I will take a turn in milking once in a while."

We headed back toward the gardens, passing the lily pond and entering a sprawling orchard containing an array of exotic-looking trees.

He stopped and looked me in the eye. There was a faint look of amusement on his face. "Now, I know you said you weren't interested in having any servants in your quarters. But wouldn't you like a female companion? Sometimes the nights can feel long without one…"

I rolled my eyes internally. Girls were the very last thing on my mind right now.

"We do have some half-blood girls who aren't yet coupled with vampires. I'd be happy to make an introduction. Just a suggestion. You are one of my people now, and it's my responsibility to make sure your needs are met…"

"I appreciate the gesture. I'll let you know," was the politest way I could think to reply to his suggestion.

We continued walking through the orchard in silence. We had almost reached the end of it when a hissing sound came from behind us. I whirled around in time to see a giant snake with jet-black scales and a blood-red tongue launch toward me.

My first instinct was to launch right back at it and tackle it to the ground. But in the split second before the snake and I made contact, Jeramiah had flown at the creature and pinned it to the floor. The snake writhed and tried to wrap around Jeramiah's body, but he kicked it to the side forcefully, holding its head from the back and positioning its gaping fangs away from him. He had a look of mild irritation on his face as he yelled out across the atrium: "Who let this snake into the orchard?"

A male vampire came hurrying out from one of the rooms on the ground level, carrying a long, thick sack. He and Jeramiah wrestled the snake into it and tied up the opening.

"Sorry about that," the vampire muttered to Jeramiah before making his way back to the room, dragging the squirming bundle behind him.

What on earth was that about?

I'd expected them to kill the creature. It might not be something a vampire couldn't handle, but it would certainly be a threat to half-bloods who weren't as strong as us. Instead they seemed to be... keeping it.

Since Jeramiah offered no explanation, I didn't ask. We exited the gardens and arrived back on the veranda that lined the ground level of the atrium.

He turned to me. "I'll have a talk with Michael and Amaya, as I said, and get back to you about other responsibilities you can take on."

I nodded. Parting ways with him, I headed straight back to my apartment.

Even aside from the fact this place was managed by Lucas Novak's son, something about this place was off... though I couldn't yet put my finger on exactly what it was.

All I know is, the sooner I get out of here, the better.

The trouble was, unless I managed to coerce a witch

into helping me, it no longer looked like I was going to get the quick escape I'd been hoping for…

CHAPTER 1: RIVER

I stared at my father through the glass separator. His black, gray-streaked hair hung limply at the sides of his face and his brown eyes looked dim and jaded. His face was speckled with more scabs than I wanted to count. His orange uniform contrasted starkly with his pale complexion and he looked thinner than I'd ever seen him. If I hadn't known him to be forty-four, I would've assumed him to be in his early sixties.

Folds of loose skin gathered on either side of his mouth as he smiled at me, revealing stained teeth. His hand unsteady, he reached for the phone on his side of the window and placed it against his ear.

I picked up the phone on my side.

"River," he breathed into the receiver, his voice raspy. "Sweetheart, how are you?"

I swallowed back the lump in my throat.

"Okay."

His eyes roamed either side of me. Then his expression sagged in disappointment.

"Dafne and Lalia… They didn't come?"

I shook my head. "I'm sorry."

He sighed heavily, then forced another smile.

"Are you off school now?"

"Yes," I replied. "We just got off two days ago."

"I've been reading whatever papers I can get a hold of, but one hasn't come my way the last week. Have there been any more kidnappings?"

"Not that I know of," I said. "The schools on the West Coast were still closed right up until the holidays started. But nobody seems sure whether the threat has passed or not."

"Well, let's hope it has passed." He paused, wetting

his lower lip. "How is your French going?"

"Spanish, Dad."

"Spanish," he said, shaking his head. "I'm sorry. How's it going?"

"Okay. I'm still a bit behind compared to the rest of the class. My teacher has given me some extra work to do over the summer."

"Good," he replied. "Good. And how are they… my three other cherubs?"

"Okay, too," I said. "Jamil is the same as ever."

The corners of my father's eyes moistened.

I broke eye contact. There was only so long I could look at him before my throat became too tight.

"When are you transferring?" I asked, staring down at the metal counter. "Still this Friday?"

"Still this Friday," he replied. "Will you come to visit me down south?"

I breathed out. "Texas is a long way, Dad… We don't have a lot of extra money right now."

"Oh, I know, honey," he said quickly. "That's okay. I'm sure we'll see each other again sometime soon…" His voice trailed off.

I looked up at the sound of his right hand pressing against the glass. He was leaning closer to look at me, clutching the phone in his left fist.

"I don't deserve you, Riv," he whispered, his voice choking up. "I don't deserve you, Dafne, Lalia, Jamil, or your mother."

That's why you lost us.

I'd heard my father say all this before. I felt numb to it now. His expressions of regret and apology had come to mean nothing to me because he never acted on them. When he was still living with us, he'd be remorseful for perhaps a couple of days, then sink back into his habit and we wouldn't see him for the next month. Although I had been devastated when my mother divorced him, I'd slowly come to realize that she'd done what was best for all of us. My father... this man... he wasn't good for us. Especially not for my younger sisters. Leaving him was the bravest thing my mother had ever done.

"I'm sorry," he said.

I wish I could believe you.

I didn't know how to respond. I still loved him more

than I could say, but he'd worn me down over the years, just as he had my mother.

But this was my last visit before his transfer and I had no idea when I'd see him again. I couldn't stand to end our meeting with bitterness or resentment. He'd made his choices, and the judge had made hers.

So I just bit my lip and nodded.

"I know, Dad."

As he leaned in toward the window further still, I wished I could touch him. Although he was a ghost of the father I remembered, a wreck of his addiction, I just wanted to feel his arms around me, his kiss against the top of my head.

I reached up to the glass, and flattened my hand against his. We remained silent in this position for several moments before a harsh voice called behind my father.

"Mr. Giovanni. You've had your time."

"Goodbye," I said softly.

My father didn't budge.

"I'm sorry, River," he repeated. "I'm so sorry."

"Mr. Remo Giovanni." The guard spoke again,

louder this time.

"Go, Dad. We'll see each other again. Hopefully soon," I said, even though I held no hope for such a thing. We were struggling just to cover our groceries. A trip across the country wouldn't be affordable for the foreseeable future.

The guard approached behind him and gripped his shoulders, pulling him back away from the window. The phone clattered against the counter. My father's wiry frame towered above the guard as he stood to his feet. His eyes remained fixed on me right up until the guard ushered him through the door.

I remained staring at the empty doorway.

Stay safe, Papa.

Chapter 2: River

Passing along the corridors toward the prison's exit, I felt like an inmate myself. I hated the way the guards eyed me, male and female. I breathed out deeply once I reached the final door and stepped out into the crisp, early evening air. I headed straight for the bus stop. There was a small crowd of people waiting there already. I took a seat on the bench as far away from everyone as possible, but I didn't manage to escape the attention of an elderly woman.

"Who were you visiting, honey?" she asked.

I wasn't in any mood to talk, but this woman had kind eyes and I didn't want to be rude.

"My father," I said quietly.

"Oh." Her face fell. "I'm so sorry, sweetie."

"That's okay."

"I came to visit my son," she said. She reached out and squeezed my hand gently. "Sometimes people just don't think through the consequences of their actions. It doesn't always mean they're bad people. Often they're just stupid… Like my dumbass boy. Smashing up a police car. What the heck was he thinking?" She shook her head.

I gave her a weak smile, then looked down at my feet.

If all my father had done was trash a vehicle, I would be sitting here now with a much lighter heart.

The woman seemed to take the hint and didn't attempt to strike up another conversation. I fumbled in my bag for my iPod, unwound the headphones from it and placed them in my ears. I brushed a finger against the cracked screen and navigated toward the files I had copied from the Spanish-learning CD my teacher had given me. I turned the volume right up, letting the soothing female voice fill my ears. It helped to drown out the thoughts going through my head.

We waited ten more minutes before a bus pulled up. After the elderly lady and the rest of the crowd had boarded, I climbed inside. I chose a seat that was furthest away from everyone and replaced my earbuds in my ears.

The bus revved and moved forward. Soon, we had started along the bridge that led back toward Long Island City. A strong gust of wind blew in through the window of the bus, catching my hair. I stared out at the river flowing beneath us. As we finished crossing the bridge, I looked behind us toward the prison one last time. I wiped my eyes against the back of my jacket sleeve as my vision blurred. Then I forced myself to focus on the Spanish in my ears once again.

I looked up again only when I sensed my stop was nearing. I thanked the driver and left the bus, stepping out onto the sidewalk. I had to wait for another fifteen minutes before the bus arrived that would take me to my next destination. I took a seat closer to the front this time, where I could get a clearer view of my surroundings. I enjoyed looking out of the window at this part of town. The pretty buildings, the fancy shops, the people wearing beautiful clothes...

I debarked again as we arrived on a particularly swanky road. Stepping out, I removed the buds from my ears and placed my iPod back in my bag. Then I straightened out my jacket and jeans so I looked a little less scruffy. I walked up to the chocolatier directly opposite the bus stop and looked at my reflection in the window. My long brown hair had gotten messy from the river wind, so I attempted to tame it a little. Once I was satisfied that I looked at least semi-presentable, I walked another hundred feet and stopped outside a gorgeous five-star hotel. Walking through the entrance, I took a left and entered the restaurant.

It was closed still, but I could see some of my colleagues milling about the tables preparing for dinner. I knocked and caught the attention of a co-worker I particularly liked—Trisha, a short young woman with curly black hair. She gave me a smile and walked over to the door. Pulling out a key from her pocket, she opened it for me.

"I didn't know you were working today," she said.

"I'm not. But I need to speak to Rachel. Is she around?"

"Yeah. She's in the kitchen doing inventory."

"Great." I hurried along the restaurant's trendy beechwood floors and entered the kitchen area round the back. Sure enough, Rachel was standing in the center of it, leaning against one of the metal counters with a tablet in her hands. As I approached, she raised her blue eyes to me, brushing aside her blonde-highlighted hair.

"River. What are you doing here?"

"Do you have a moment?" I asked, setting my heavy bag down on one of the tabletops.

"Sure," she said.

"As I told you, I won't be able to work next week. But when I return, I wanted to ask if there are any extra slots you could give me, say… starting Monday the twenty-fourth?"

She furrowed her brows. "You're already scheduled to work lunch and dinner, five days a week. You really want to work on weekends too? It's the summer holidays."

Exactly. I had to work as much as I could before school started up again.

"Yes. I'd like to take as many extra days as you have available. Can you fit me in?"

"Hm. I s'pose I could schedule you on Saturdays too."

"Thank you," I said.

"Was that all you came to see me about?"

"Yes." I picked up my bag and flung it back over my shoulder. "Have a good evening."

"You too, hon," she said, giving me another smile before looking back down at her tablet.

I headed back out onto the street and hopped onto another bus. The prospect of a day of extra income per week had lightened my mood a little. I plugged myself back into the calm voice of the Spanish woman. As the last leg of my journey progressed, I became increasingly grateful for her calm, because the bus got delayed a number of times before reaching my neighborhood. My mother would be worrying and wondering why I was late. And my phone battery had died, which meant I couldn't call her. The thought of my mother worrying always made me tense.

When the elegant roads gave way to shabbier, rougher-looking ones, I knew I was nearing home. It was dark by the time the bus finally pulled up at my stop. I took a moment to tuck my bag beneath my jacket and pull up the hood over my head before racing along the shadowy sidewalk toward our apartment block. Only lost tourists were out after dark on these streets. When I had a late shift cleaning up in the restaurant kitchen, Trisha usually let me crash at her place and return home in the morning so I didn't have to make the journey at night.

At the entrance to our towering apartment block, two hooded men smoked by the doorway. I fixed my eyes on the ground and strode through the door. I walked to the far corner of the entry area where the mailboxes were stacked. Pulling the key from my bag's zip pocket, I opened our box. There was only one letter inside. A thin brown envelope addressed to Nadia Haik.

It was still strange to see my mother being addressed by her maiden name, even though it had been more than two years now since the divorce. I slipped the letter into my bag, locked the box and hurried past the elevator toward the stairs. I never used the elevator anymore, not since it had broken down on me six months ago and I'd been trapped in it alone for two hours before the engineer came.

I climbed up staircase after staircase until I reached the seventh floor. Panting, I leaned against the wall to catch my breath. The smell of delicious cooking wafted into my nostrils. It made me realize how hungry I was.

I ran the rest of the distance to the door of our two-bedroom apartment and opened it with my key.

"River?" My mother's voice drifted through from the kitchen as I shut the door behind me.

"Hello, Mom," I called back, untying my shoes.

She appeared in the hallway wearing an apron, her thick brown hair tied up in a bun. She placed her hands on her waist, her turquoise eyes wide.

"What happened? I tried to call you."

"Sorry. My phone battery died." I finished taking off

my shoes and stood up straight. At five-seven, I was two inches taller than my mother.

"How come you're almost an hour late?"

"I got delayed on the bus journey home." I reached into my bag for her letter and handed it to her. She took it from me and eyed it briefly before looking back at me. I could see the question behind her eyes, but I knew she'd wait until my sisters had gone to bed.

"You must be starving." She took my hand and led me into the kitchen. I dumped my bag on the floor. My three siblings were still seated at the table in the center of the small room.

"Why are you so late, River?" Lalia, my six-year-old sister, scolded through a mouthful of hummus.

I heaved a sigh and sat down at the table. "The buses weren't behaving themselves."

My ten-year-old sister Dafne peered at me through her round purple spectacles. "Where did you go?"

"You know… the restaurant."

Dafne, Lalia and I looked more like our mother than our father—more Lebanese than Italian. We shared her eye color, her rich brown hair and light tan skin. My nineteen-year-old brother sitting opposite me resembled our father uncannily with his black hair, brown eyes and whiter skin tone.

"Hello, Jamil," I said, giving him a smile.

He gave me a lopsided half-smile and met my gaze briefly before mumbling inaudibly to himself and looking down at the table. I could see that my mother had been feeding him when I'd arrived back—he had half a plate of stuffed eggplant and falafel still in front of him.

My mother approached with my plate and set it down in front of me. My mouth watering, I dug right in. There was nothing in the world like my mom's cooking. She resumed her seat next to Jamil, picked up his fork and continued feeding him.

"How's the makdous?" she asked. "I think I added too little salt."

"No, it's perfect," I said. "So what have you guys been up to today?"

"We've just been hanging around the apartment… Dafne's been getting a headstart on her history homework—"

"Hey, River, you know my class is studying the Ancient Egyptians next year?" Dafne interrupted. "Finally!"

I chuckled. Our grandfather on my mother's side being an Egyptologist, I wouldn't have been surprised if Dafne knew more about Egyptian history than her history teacher.

"And Lalia painted a picture," my mother continued.

"Of us!" Lalia piped up. Still clutching a piece of falafel in one hand, she slid off her seat and ran out of the kitchen. She returned with a watercolor painting. It was typical Lalia-style—brave, bold colors and half a dozen giant flowers floating around our stick figures for no discernible reason. This wasn't the first family portrait Lalia had painted. We had a whole pile of them stacked beneath her bed. But something about this one made me stop chewing.

Our father was missing. This was the first painting I'd seen of hers where she'd excluded him.

Although it made me ache inside, I supposed it was a good thing. Perhaps she was letting go. I caught my mother's eye. From the look of melancholy on her face, I could tell that she was thinking the same thing.

"It's beautiful, Laly," I said, kissing her chubby cheek.

She grinned proudly before setting the picture down on the kitchen counter and resuming her seat between Dafne and my mother.

"We also made baklava," my mother said.

"Can I have some?" Lalia said, stuffing the last forkful of her main course into her mouth.

My mother rolled her eyes. "You already sneaked five pieces before dinner, little rascal."

"Just one... please?" Lalia fluttered her eyelashes.

"I'll give you half a piece," my mother muttered, standing up and opening the fridge door.

Lalia pulled her grumpy face.

"Baklava will start coming out of your ears soon if you're not careful," Dafne said, casting Lalia a sideways glance.

My mother returned with a tray of the sweet, rich pastry. Slicing a piece in half, she handed it to Lalia. Then she scooped up two pieces and handed them to

Dafne and placed two pieces in a bowl for me before putting the tray back in the fridge.

"None for Jamil?" Dafne asked.

My mother shook her head. "I'm cutting down on his sugar for a while. It's not good for him."

I finished the last of my savory food and pushed my chair back, rubbing my stomach. I was stuffed.

"Oh, and Grandpa called," my mother continued. "Dafne spoke to him."

"What did he say?" I asked, leaning forward.

"He just wanted to make sure we were ready for the trip," Dafne replied. "And he said he's got a surprise for us when we arrive."

My grandfather always had one surprise or another for us when we went to visit in the summer. He lived in Cairo. Dafne, Lalia and I were due to travel there this coming Sunday—without my mother. She'd had a falling out with her father a few months ago.

"He also said again how disappointed he is that we're only going for a week this time," Dafne continued.

"Yeah." I breathed out. "Well, I already told him I

want to work more this summer. You two could stay on longer than me. Bashira could bring you back… I'm sure Grandpa wouldn't mind the expense."

"You can discuss it with him when you arrive," my mother said. She eyed Lalia and Dafne, who'd both finished dessert by now. "Okay, time for bed."

Lalia crinkled her nose. "But it's summer break."

"And you've already stayed up an hour past your usual bedtime. Come."

Lalia leapt up from her chair and darted into the living room, while Dafne obediently made her way to the bathroom to brush her teeth.

My mother chased after Lalia and returned to the kitchen half a minute later, carrying my sister on her back. "River, could you keep an eye on Jamil while I put this monkey to bed?"

Jamil's head lolled slightly as he sat strapped to his chair. He'd be ready to sleep soon.

"Yeah," I said, standing up and walking to the sink.

"When are you coming to bed, River?" Lalia called to me as my mother disappeared with her toward the bathroom.

"Soon," I called back.

I started washing up the plates and cutlery from dinner.

Jamil grunted suddenly. I whirled around to see his shoulders beginning to tremble. Dropping the plates in the sink, I ran to the kitchen door and unhooked the helmet that hung over the back of it. I strapped it over his head and fastened it just in time before his whole body went into a seizure. If he hadn't been strapped to the chair, he would have fallen to the floor.

After his body had stopped shaking so violently, his hands balled into fists and he reached for his head as he attempted to hit himself over and over again. Unstrapping him from the chair, I caught both of his hands gently and helped him to his feet. He continued struggling against me as he tried to punch himself. He was taller and stronger than me, but I was practiced at this by now. I guided both of his hands behind his back and held them there firmly, but gently.

"It's okay, Jamil," I said softly, resting my cheek against his back. "I've got you."

His groaning and grunting trailed off and he

stopped struggling so hard to free his hands. Once I was sure that he wasn't going to attempt to hit himself again, I slowly let go of him. Although he was unrestrained, both hands remained exactly as I'd positioned them behind his back.

I slipped an arm around his waist and led him out of the kitchen toward the bathroom. I could hear my mother now in the second bedroom, reading a story to Dafne and Lalia. I entered the bathroom with Jamil, pulled down the toilet lid and sat him down. I removed his helmet, then picked up his toothbrush and helped him to brush his teeth. Then I assisted him in changing into his nightclothes. Once he was ready, I led him to the bedroom he shared with my mother. Although it was a small room, she had to sleep in there in case he needed assistance during the night. I guided Jamil into bed—the left of the two twin beds lined up on opposite sides of the room—and pulled up his blanket.

The seizure he'd had was the strongest I'd seen in a while. He looked exhausted by it. I held his hand until his eyelids closed and his breathing became steady. It didn't take long, only five minutes. My mother had finished reading to my sisters by the time I came out and was finishing cleaning up the kitchen.

"Jamil's sleeping?" she asked as I entered.

"Yes. He just had a fit."

"Oh, dear. That's the fifth one today."

We were both quiet as my mom finished washing up. Then we headed into the living room and took a seat on the couch.

"So," she started, her voice low, "how did it go with your father?"

"How could it have possibly gone? He said he was sorry. I said goodbye. He wasn't given long."

My mother nodded, biting her lower lip. "Was he disappointed Dafne and Lalia didn't come?"

"Of course."

"Did he understand why they didn't?"

"He seemed to."

My mother paused. "Did he ask you to visit him?"

"Yes. I told him I couldn't promise anything."

She leaned back on the sofa, heaving a sigh. I drew up my feet and wrapped my arms around my knees.

"Lalia seems to have accepted the situation," my

mother said. "But Dafne keeps asking me where he is. I'm not sure what to say to her anymore. I just... I don't want to hurt her."

"Dafne's mature for her age," I said. "It might be time to just tell her the truth."

Tears burned in my mother's eyes. But she swallowed hard and held them back. "Next time she asks, I'll tell her." She breathed in deeply. "So, are you looking forward to going to Grandpa's?"

"Yeah. I mean it will just be like always. It's nice to have a break there, but... Mom, I'm so worried about how you will cope here all alone with Jamil."

"Don't think of me," she said. "You just go and enjoy yourself. I'll manage."

I snuggled closer on the couch, resting my head against her shoulder. I doubted I'd be able to pass more than an hour without worrying about her here in this apartment.

She wrapped an arm around me and pulled me closer, brushing my forehead with her other hand. We remained silent in each other's company for a couple of minutes before she reached for the remote and switched on the TV.

She began flipping through the channels, and stopped at a news channel.

"They're still talking about these kidnappings," she said. "I just can't believe on some channels they're bouncing around words like 'vampires' and 'witches'... I mean, I'm talking about respectable newscasters here. They're supposed to be delivering news, not spreading hoaxes. The footage they're showing seems realistic— but so do sci-fi movies these days. It's nothing a skilled special-effects team couldn't pull off."

"That footage of the attack in Chile," I said. "You can actually see the man ripping into the person's throat... And what about that dragon footage shot in California? Why would someone want to create an elaborate hoax like this? And what do you think is the cause of these attacks and kidnappings? What about all the missing people, and the witnesses?"

"I have no clue. I was hoping one of these news channels could finally shine some light rather than continue to spout this recycled crap... Seems I hoped for too much."

"They even closed the schools along the West Coast," I muttered.

"Well, some dreadful organized crime is clearly going on here. Whoever's behind this seems to be having fun leaving this media frenzy after them to cover their tracks."

I'd never witnessed such bizarre theories being broadcast around mainstream media. This was the type of thing you'd read about on sketchy conspiracy blogs. Of course, my mother was right. These media conglomerates were just spinning this story to get more views and sell more papers.

Witches didn't exist.

And vampires certainly didn't.

Chapter 3: River

The next few days passed quickly until our trip. Before we knew it, it was the night before and my sisters and I were finishing our packing.

I was kneeling in the bedroom I shared with Dafne and Lalia, making sure my purse contained all the important documents we needed—all three of our passports and other travel documents. My mother would come with us in a taxi to drop us off at the airport, and our grandfather would be waiting at the other end to pick us up. I'd made this journey several times before with my mother, and was used to it. Besides, the airport staff was always helpful if I wasn't sure where to go with my sisters.

"You should put Lalia's inhaler in your bag," my mother called from the hallway.

Lalia's asthma was better than it had been a few years ago, but there were still occasions when she needed her inhaler.

My little sister was lounging on her bed, humming an off-tune song to herself as she busied herself with a coloring book.

"Laly, where's your inhaler?" I asked.

"I dunno," she mumbled, making no motion to get up and look for it.

I guessed my mother had put it in the bathroom cupboard. I was right. Pulling it out, I placed it in my backpack.

We went to bed early that night because we were due to leave at 4am the following morning. The three of us woke up to my shrill alarm going off. Stumbling out of bed, we crowded into the bathroom. Lalia was falling asleep standing up, her toothbrush hanging lopsided in her mouth. I grabbed a washcloth and wet it with cold water, brushing it over her face to wake her up.

We took turns taking a shower and getting dressed. My mother was already in the kitchen, making sandwiches for us to take to the airport.

Once the taxi driver called up to say that he had arrived, I bundled out of the apartment with my two sisters and our luggage, while my mother made her way down after us with Jamil strapped into his wheelchair. I took the stairs while the rest of them took their chances with the elevator.

Arriving on the ground floor, we stepped outside and piled into the car. As it drove away, I couldn't help but feel excitement for the journey. Although I wished that my mother and Jamil could come with us, I couldn't deny that I would enjoy getting out of the neighborhood for a while.

Once we had arrived at the airport, my mother and Jamil stayed with us as long as they could until we got in line for the security checks. Then we kissed and said goodbye before my sisters and I passed through the barrier into departures.

We kept waving until my mother was out of sight. I looked down at my two sisters. Lalia was wide-eyed and looking around at the shops surrounding us in the departure lounge, clutching my forefinger in her pudgy hand. Dafne was looking up at me expectantly.

"What now?" she asked.

I took her hand too, holding both of my sisters close to me, and checked the departures board.

"We don't have that long to wait. Half an hour before we have to go to our gate. We can hang around the shops."

We couldn't afford to purchase anything, but my sisters enjoyed looking around the perfume shop. After that, we moved to the book shop and spent the rest of our time there before heading to the gate for boarding.

Lalia requested her sandwich and finished it during the fifteen minutes we had to hang around before we could finally board the plane. We took seats next to each other near the front of the aircraft. Dafne got air sickness so she got the window seat, while I positioned Lalia in the middle and I sat in the aisle seat.

A mischievous smile slowly spread across Lalia's face. She looked up at me. "Did Mommy pack any lollipops… or baklava?"

"No baklava," I replied, rolling my eyes. "But she gave us lollipops to help keep our ears unblocked. I'll give you one once the flight takes off."

I handed her and Dafne a strawberry lollipop as the plane took off from the runway and unwrapped one for myself too. I leaned back in my chair, looking up at the screen above our seats. We had a long flight ahead of us.

After Dafne and I ate our sandwiches, all three of us fell asleep. It was lunchtime by the time I woke up again. An air stewardess was standing by our row of seats, offering us trays of food.

I woke my sisters and placed our tables down in front of us. We watched a movie as we ate, and after lunch, Dafne and I played a game of hangman while Lalia continued watching the screen. Once the movie had finished, Lalia insisted on playing a game of snap—my mother had thoughtfully packed the cards in her bag. It was one of her favorite games, and she won almost all the time.

We dozed off again at some point and, on waking up the next time, it was to the news that we were approaching Cairo International Airport. I felt the plane beginning to descend. I looked over at Dafne. She was staring out the window, her knuckles pale as she gripped her seat. Surprisingly, she had coped well on this journey. Normally she vomited at least once.

Once the plane had touched down and taxied to a stop, we all stood up and stretched our legs. Then I bundled our carry on luggage out of the locker overhead. I felt excited as we moved toward the front of the plane. It wouldn't be long now until we would be reunited with our grandfather.

As we stepped out of the plane, the hot Egyptian air engulfed us. I was already sweating. We hurried through the rest of the airport and, after reclaiming our baggage, we finally reached the arrivals area. We looked around for our grandfather. Lalia was the one who spotted him first.

"Grandpa!"

He was a short man with white hair and a beard that

covered half his face. He wore a light cotton suit, and his tan face split into a smile as he spotted us.

"My girls!"

We rushed into his arms and he cuddled all three of us at once. The smell of his cologne filled my nostrils.

"How was the flight?" he asked, his Lebanese accent thick as ever.

"It went smoothly," I said.

A tall ebony-skinned man arrived next to him. "Meet Fariss," my grandfather said. "My new driver."

Fariss smiled and shook hands with each of us. He bent down and picked up my sisters' luggage. When he motioned to carry mine too, I held up a hand and said, "No, it's fine. I can manage. Thanks."

We made our way toward my grandfather's shiny black car in the parking lot. My sisters and I sat in the back while our grandfather sat in the passenger seat. After Fariss had packed all the luggage into the back, he started up the engine and drove us away.

I reached for a paper napkin stuffed into the back of one of the seats and wiped my forehead.

"Wow, it's hot," I said.

"Welcome to Cairo." My grandfather chuckled.

"So what's the surprise, Grandpa?" Dafne asked.

He swiveled in his seat to look back at us, a gleam in his eyes. "Well, it didn't look like it was going to coincide with your visit at first, but plans changed… We've been invited to an exciting dig. It's in the ruins of an ancient temple and it's happening in the desert not too far from home."

"Oh, my," Dafne gasped.

"Normally they wouldn't allow children to attend such things, but the organizer is a friend of mine and he agreed to make an exception. So… what do you say?"

"Yes!" Dafne squealed.

Lalia still looked too overwhelmed by the change of scenery and temperature to register what my grandfather was saying. She was staring out of the window. I was sure that he would find a way to make the dig interesting even for a six-year-old.

The dig certainly sounded exciting to me. Although I wasn't quite as much of a nerd as Dafne when it came to Egyptian history, I was always interested in my grandfather's work.

"How long will the dig last?" I asked.

"Well, it's started already. But I think we will most likely see something interesting by the day after tomorrow. I suggest we leave early, stay the whole day and night and return the next day before lunchtime."

"Stay the night? In the desert?" Dafne looked all the more excited by the prospect.

"Yes. They've set up camp there."

"Wow," Dafne said.

"Bashira would come with us, too," my grandfather added.

"How is Bashira?" I asked. My grandmother had died five years ago, and now my grandfather lived alone except for his longtime housekeeper, Bashira.

"Her joints are getting a bit stiff, but otherwise she's in good spirits. She's very much looking forward to seeing you three again." He paused, straining his neck to look me in the eye. "Are you really going to go back after just one week? I'm still sore about it."

"Dafne and Lalia could stay longer… then perhaps Bashira could fly back with them to New York?"

My grandfather turned his attention to my two sisters. "And would you two like to do that? Stay here without River?"

Dafne nodded her head furiously. "Can I stay a whole month?"

"Of course! And what about you, Lalia?"

She tore her eyes away from the window. "Huh?"

"Grandpa's asking if you want to stay here longer with Dafne," I said. "I'll be returning home after a week."

She paused, looking from me to our grandfather. "Ummm, I'll stay for just... four more days if River isn't gonna be there."

"Just four more days?" my grandfather said, chuckling. "I like how precise you are. Okay, I'll change the tickets when we get home."

After half an hour, we pulled up in the dusty street outside my grandfather's home. It was a five-bedroom house—not including Bashira's quarters, which were round the back—and beautifully constructed. Its white exterior and sleek stone entryway made it seem like a miniature palace.

We entered through the heavy door and looked around at the entrance hall. The walls were covered with parchment containing hieroglyphics, mounted in gold frames. Ancient relics from his various excursions covered the long mantelpiece. We approached the wide staircase in the center of the room and my grandfather led us up.

"So, where would you like to sleep? You have four bedrooms up here to choose from."

Dafne chose the room with the best view of the swimming pool in the back garden. Lalia just looked up at me. "Where you gonna sleep, River?" she asked.

"Umm..." I looked around the three remaining rooms and chose the one closest to Dafne's, also with the view of the backyard and the pool. "Let's sleep in this one."

"Well, if you want to make yourselves comfortable... Are you hungry or sleepy?" my grandfather asked.

Since we had slept on the plane, none of us were tired. We'd also eaten quite a lot. After we greeted Bashira, a kind Egyptian woman in her late fifties, she served us iced watermelon juice and fresh dates. Then we spent time with my grandfather in his library.

Although his living room was comfortable, his library also contained a large sofa, and it was by far the most interesting room in the house. Its walls were covered with ceiling-high bookcases filled with hundreds of books about Egypt. Dafne could sit in here for hours and hours flying through pages. I was sure that she would become an Egyptologist when she grew up. My grandfather was certainly hoping for it.

We retired to bed once our eyelids started drooping. Lalia and I awoke the next morning to a delicious smell wafting into our bedroom. We padded into the ensuite bathroom, brushed our teeth and took showers. We both changed into our swimsuits and pulled on light cotton dresses from the cupboard that Bashira had bought especially for us. Then we headed downstairs to find Bashira in the midst of cooking a traditional Egyptian breakfast. We helped her finish preparing the meal and then set up the breakfast table outside in the backyard. Dafne and my grandfather joined us within half an hour. After filling our bellies, we lounged around by the pool. I could hardly remember the last time I'd been swimming. I supposed it was the last time I'd visited here.

"For dinner, I have a suggestion," my grandfather said, looking down at us in the pool as he sat in a deck chair. "My friend, Yusuf, the organizer of the dig, has invited us to a lovely Lebanese restaurant about twenty minutes away. I might have taken you all there before, actually, the last time you came with your mother and Jamil… They also serve a certain sweet pastry that some people around here are fond of…"

I laughed as Lalia stopped swimming and perked up. "Baklava?" she asked, wide-eyed.

"Yes." My grandfather grinned. "Yusuf has a son around your age, River—Hassan is his name."

"Sounds fun," I said, swimming to the edge of the pool and climbing out. I grabbed my towel and sat down in a chair, watching my sisters as they continued splashing in the water.

We spent the rest of the day in the backyard with my grandfather. Dafne and Lalia stopped swimming only for a light lunch, and soon enough, it was time to get ready for dinner.

I headed with Lalia back to our bedroom. We rummaged through the array of beautiful clothes Bashira had bought for us. Lalia picked out a light pink cotton dress. I helped her change into it, then tied her hair back in a French braid.

"I'm *real* pretty," Lalia said, checking herself out in the mirror and swinging her long braid from side to side.

"You *are*," I said, smiling. *And oh so modest, too.*

"Why don't you wear that purple one?" she asked, pointing to a long flowing gown.

I eyed it. "Meh. Purple isn't really my color." I opted for a dark blue dress instead. It was long but sleeveless, and had a cooling feel to it. I brushed out my hair and was about to tie it up in a bun when Lalia reached for my hand. "It looks nice down."

I paused, looking at myself in the mirror. She was right that it looked better down. It was just so long that it got in the way—I was in the habit of tying it up all the time. Still, this was a special occasion, so I took my little sister's suggestion.

Once Lalia and I were ready, we left the bedroom and went downstairs. My grandfather and Dafne were ready and waiting for us. Dafne had chosen a pretty green gown that complemented her purple glasses.

"Well?" my grandfather said. "Are we ready to leave, princesses?"

"Yep," I replied.

We left the house and walked down the steps toward the car. Fariss was already waiting by it. He opened the door to the back seats and my sisters and I climbed inside, while my grandfather sat in the front. The restaurant wasn't far away, as my grandfather had said. Soon we were pulling up outside a familiar building. Its exposed brick exterior had an ethnic charm and deep blue fabric draped down from pillars that lined the restaurant's terrace. This restaurant was right on the edge of town and it had a stunning view of the desert—indeed, the sand started just twenty feet from the entrance.

"Are you hungry, Fariss? You should join us," my father said.

"I have eaten already," he replied. "But thank you

for the invitation."

"Then you don't need to wait around here if you've other things to do. We'll be here at least a couple of hours. Why don't you aim to return by nine-thirty?"

"Yes, sir."

We left Fariss with the car and walked into the restaurant. It was adorned with beautiful bamboo furniture and cozy lanterns dangled from the ceiling. It was more crowded than I'd expected. We walked up to the woman standing behind the welcome desk.

"Do you have a reservation?" she asked.

"Yes. My name is Samir Haik, and my two friends…" His voice trailed off as his eyes fixed on two men sitting in the far corner of the room—at one of the tables with the best views of the desert. "I see they've arrived already."

"Enjoy your evening," the woman said.

We headed toward the table and the father and son stood up when they spotted us. Yusuf had graying black hair, a thick mustache and tan skin. He positively towered over my short grandfather. Hassan looked like a younger version of his father. He also had a mustache, albeit much less salubrious than Yusuf's.

"Samir!" Yusuf said, grinning. He grabbed my grandfather's hand and pulled him in for a hug. Then he turned to the rest of us. "And who are these angels?"

"Meet Lalia, Dafne, and River," my grandfather said, gesturing to each of us.

We shook hands with him, then Hassan, who smiled more broadly as he met my eye.

"A pleasure to meet you," he said, his Middle Eastern accent thick.

"And you too," I said politely.

I wasn't sure whether it was just my imagination, but my grandfather and Yusuf seemed to deliberately engineer the seating so that I was next to Hassan.

After we'd scanned the menus and chosen what we wanted, the waitress came to take orders. For the first half of the meal, we listened to my grandfather and Yusuf speaking enthusiastically about the dig—how long they had been planning for it and trying to get permission, how they had finally succeeded and how it had been going so far. Apparently they had already discovered some artifacts of interest.

It was only after about forty-five minutes that Hassan spoke to me again.

"My father tells me you are from New York?" he asked, glancing at me curiously.

I swallowed my mouthful of salad. "Yes," I said. "Manhattan."

"I have visited there once with my parents. I found it a nice place."

"Yes, parts of it are nice," I replied.

"How long are you staying here in Cairo?" he asked.

"Just a week this time."

"Oh, I see…" He looked across the table at my two sisters. "You are not here with your parents?"

"No." The thought of my father in a Texas jail and my mother stuck in our apartment with my autistic brother suddenly made the food in my mouth tasteless. I worried about how my mother was even going to sort out basic things like groceries.

"Do you live in Cairo full-time?" I asked Hassan, eager to change the subject.

"Yes."

"Where are you from originally?"

"Born and raised in Cairo," he replied proudly. "Were you born in the United States?"

"Yes. Though my mother was born in Egypt."

Our conversation trailed off and we went back to listening to my grandfather and Yusuf's discussion.

Lalia and Dafne were busy eating. They'd worked up a good appetite from all the swimming they'd done earlier. I caught myself wondering whether Lalia would even have room for any dessert, then reminded myself that she *always* had room for dessert.

Once we'd finished, the waitress took away our dinner plates and we ordered dessert. Lalia requested the obvious, while the rest of us opted for ice cream. Hassan chose the same flavor as me—mango.

Once we'd finished, Yusuf insisted on paying the check. Then we all retreated to the sitting area outside on the veranda and admired the view of the desert. Lalia and Dafne both looked drowsy by now as they slumped back in a sofa. I stretched out my legs next to them, yawning and looking up at the starry night sky and then straight ahead at the endless mass of dunes. A cool breeze wafted over us.

As my grandfather and Yusuf immersed themselves in conversation once again, Hassan gestured with his head toward the dunes. "Shall we take a short walk?" he asked.

I felt so full, I wasn't really in the mood for a walk, but the desert did look beautiful in the moonlight.

"Grandpa," I said, standing up and interrupting his conversation. "Hassan and I are going to go for a short walk. We won't go far."

"Okay," he said. "But be careful."

Neither Lalia nor Dafne made any move to come with us. They were too full. So Hassan and I left the sitting area together and descended the veranda steps. Grains of sand filled my shoes as soon as we reached the bottom. We walked slowly forward. Now that we were away from the shelter of the veranda, the breeze was stronger.

"Watch out for snakes," Hassan said suddenly.

I jolted back. "Snakes?"

"Yes. Cobras. They tend to come out at night." He reached for my hand and pulled me closer to him.

Oh. Nice move. I rolled my eyes.

We remained close to the streetlights that bordered the desert as we ventured further along the sand.

"Have you gone with your father on a lot of digs?" I asked.

"Yes."

"Will you be there tomorrow also?"

"Oh, certainly," he said, smiling.

"I've never stayed the night in a desert before. Do you have any advice about what I should pack?"

He thought for a moment, then shook his head. "Not really. The camp is well-stocked. Plenty of water and even toilet accessories. You'll find packets of toothbrushes, toothpaste, soap, shampoo… pretty much everything a man or woman could need. The tents are also very comfortable—and spacious. The toilets are a little walk away, however—the only real inconvenient thing about the experience."

"I see."

Hassan averted his eyes away from me again, and stopped in his tracks.

"You see something over there?" he said, squinting as he stared into the distance.

I followed his gaze. I walked closer, straining to see. If my eyes weren't mistaken, they were tanks. And there was a crowd of people surrounding them.

"They're tanks, aren't they?" he said.

"Looks like it," I replied. "I guess they're from the army?"

"I guess so. They just seem to be standing around and talking. Shall we move closer and see?"

I looked back toward the restaurant, now quite far behind us, and then back at the tanks. They weren't all that much further. I shrugged. "Okay."

As we moved closer, I heard voices more clearly. I'd been expecting to hear Arabic, but to my surprise, it sounded like the crowd of men were American. Before we were close enough to make sense of what they were saying, two of the men left the crowd and approached us. They wore dark beige uniforms and thick belts around their waists held an array of odd objects. Each carried a boxlike device with a red flashing light, a sharp spear-like weapon carved from wood and a silver gun with an odd bulbous barrel.

"Can we help you?" one of the men asked, his voice

gruff.

Hassan looked taken aback. "We were curious as to what you're doing out here."

"It's nothing you need to concern yourself about."

There wasn't anything Hassan or I could think of to respond to that. I looked past the men toward the crowd behind them, now all silent and looking us over, before we backed away and took our leave.

"Americans," Hassan muttered once we were out of earshot. "Odd." He was quiet for the next minute as he pondered it over, then shrugged it off and pointed back to the restaurant. "Shall we return? They might be starting to worry."

I agreed that was a good idea. I was still feeling nervous about cobras.

Dafne and Lalia looked a bit more lively as we returned. They sat cross-legged on either side of a coffee table and were playing snap. Dafne must have brought it with her in her bag.

"Did you have a nice walk?" my grandfather asked.

"Yes," I said. "We came across a group of American soldiers, or so they seemed to be, standing by a bunch of tanks."

"Americans?" he asked, raising his eyebrows.

"Yes," Hassan replied. "We approached to see what they were up to but they gave us a non-answer."

"That is odd," Yusuf said, looking out toward the desert. "Hopefully it's nothing to worry about."

We speculated some more about the American soldiers, then decided to call it a night and left the restaurant. Fariss was already waiting outside for us.

"Well," my grandfather said, hugging Yusuf and Hassan, "we will see you early tomorrow."

My sisters and I shook hands with Yusuf and Hassan, then got in the car. Lalia had fallen asleep by the time we reached home. She was heavy for her age, but with the help of Fariss and my grandfather, we lifted her out of the car. I shook her gently.

"Laly, get on my back," I said.

She opened her eyes drowsily, then I helped her climb on my back and we entered the house. I headed straight for our bedroom and insisted that she brush her teeth before falling into bed. I was feeling hot and sweaty, so I took a shower and changed into a nightgown before joining Lalia on the mattress.

I lay on my back and stared up at the ceiling, my sister's snoring in my ears.

I thought about the dig tomorrow, then about my mother, my brother, and my father, but for some reason as I drifted off to sleep that night, it was those odd American soldiers we'd found in the desert who were on my mind.

CHAPTER 4: RIVER

It was the day we were due to leave for the dig and we had to get an early start. Yusuf and Hassan would be pulling up outside at 8am sharp. We didn't have time for breakfast, so after we had washed, dressed and packed up some belongings, we headed downstairs. Bashira had prepared some containers of hot food for the journey, but apparently there would be plenty of food once we arrived at the site. There was a large caravan that served as a kitchen and dining room, according to my grandfather.

Yusuf and Hassan pulled up in a black car exactly on time. We all transferred to my grandfather's shiny white truck, Fariss in the driver's seat. Soon we'd reached the end of the roads and Fariss began driving the truck over the sand. After half an hour of the bumpy landscape, I was feeling sick. I fixed my eyes straight ahead through the windshield. We had to close all the windows and put the AC on because the sand was flying in.

By the time we arrived at the site, it was noon. The first thing we saw was a spread of large dark green tents erected on a raised area of sand. Arriving at the top gave us full view of the entire camp. Up close, the tents looked sturdy and secure. They were made of thick material that withstood the desert wind. There were also long caravans parked here and there, and I spotted a toilet sign at the very edge of the camp, away from the tents. There were wooden tables fixed into the sand and digging equipment scattered everywhere as people wearing hats and long-sleeved shirts milled about large holes that had been dug into the ground. I made sure my sisters were wearing their hats and headscarves that

Bashira had provided as we climbed out from the vehicle and looked around.

"Let's get set up in the tents first," Yusuf said. "This way."

We followed him toward the cluster of tents. He entered the third one that we passed. It was much larger inside than I'd expected. It contained five spacious compartments that were to be our bedrooms while we stayed here. They were comfortable looking, with mattresses on the ground, covered with clean white linens and pillows. Each compartment also contained a cabinet filled with snacks and lots of bottled water.

"As you see, you have a room each," Yusuf said.

We dumped our stuff in the tent and then walked back outside.

"Girls," my grandfather said, pointing to the group of static caravans in the distance. "The toilets are over there. They have showers there too."

I needed to use the bathroom, so I went there with my sisters. It was surprisingly clean inside. The floors were stark white, as were the rest of the furnishings.

We used the bathroom, washed our hands and then splashed our faces with water. It had been a long, sticky journey.

When we exited the caravan and crossed the baking-hot sand dunes, my grandfather and Yusuf had already joined the diggers and were overseeing the work they were doing.

"Over here, girls," my grandfather said on spotting us. He pointed to a wide wooden table that had been fixed in the sand. It was covered with stone objects and ancient-looking artifacts.

"This is everything we've unearthed so far that is of interest," Yusuf said, looking over the table with fascination.

Dafne's eyes positively lit up as she gazed down at the stone carving of what looked like an eye. She began talking animatedly with my grandfather, while I took Lalia's hand and we ventured further into the dig site, snaking around holes and looking down at the people digging there. Lalia asked me countless questions—what the names were of the tools they were using, how deep they were going to dig, if there were any snakes or scorpions around—and I tried to answer as best as I could. I kept looking at her and smiling. She didn't know how cute she looked in her headscarf and oversized sunglasses. I had left my phone in the tent, but I made a note to take a picture of her to show to our mother when we returned.

We wandered around the rest of the site until 2:30pm when it was time for lunch. We headed to a particularly large caravan about half a mile away from the main tent area and, entering, found a long dining table. A delicious aroma wafted toward us from the kitchens round the back. We all sat down to eat and then everyone headed back outside to continue work. We remained outside until evening, and Hassan, my sisters and I even had a go at unearthing some artifacts ourselves under my grandfather's supervision. As night began to fall, we headed back to the large table where all the artifacts had been piled up. It was fascinating to see everything together in one place.

People had started building a bonfire about thirty feet away from the tents, and Hassan beckoned me over to sit down beside him. My sisters, grandfather,

Yusuf and a whole crowd of people gathered round the fire. I was surprised when Yusuf pulled out a giant sack of marshmallows. Soon we were all toasting marshmallows while sipping date and banana smoothies.

We chatted around the fire until about 9pm. By this time, my head was beginning to feel strangely light. I clasped a palm to my forehead. It felt hot. I must've stayed outside too long today. I wasn't used to this heat. I felt like I was coming down with a migraine. I set down my empty cup on the sand and backed away from the fire, which was hot against my face.

"What's wrong, River?" Hassan asked.

"I think I'll make it an early night. I have a headache."

"You should return to the tent and drink lots of water," my grandfather said.

Yeah, and then need the toilet all night long...

I looked toward Lalia. "Are you coming to bed now? Or will you come later with Dafne?"

She was already standing up and walking over to me. She clutched my hand. "I'll come now," she said. Her cheeks were bright red. I felt her forehead—it felt hot too. Her breathing was unsteady.

"Are you okay?" I asked. "Do you need your inhaler?"

"I think I'm okay," she said, a little too breathlessly.

"Come on, let's go back… Good night," I called to everyone sitting around the fire.

"Good night," they called back, many of whom I hadn't even spoken to yet.

We returned to our tent and stepped into our compartment. The first thing I did was look for Lalia's inhaler. I prepared it, then watched as she breathed in. Her breathing returned to normal after that.

"Feel better?" I asked.

"Yeah," she mumbled.

"Now, before we sleep, do you need the toilet?"

"Erm…" She bit her lip and narrowed her eyes in concentration. "Nope."

I sighed. *I've heard that before.*

Although my head was beginning to feel like an oven, I decided to take her to the bathroom anyway. Rather now than in the middle of the night. We moved away from the tents and crossed the stretch of sand toward the ladies' toilets. We walked inside the caravan to find it empty. It turned out that Lalia really didn't need to go, so we soon made our way back to the tent. I took it for granted that she would want to share my compartment, so I led her into it and zipped us inside.

"You don't look so well, River," Lalia said, looking at me in the dim lighting of the electric lamp at the end of my mattress.

"I'll be fine in the morning," I muttered, lying down.

Lalia settled down next to me and after a few minutes, I'd fallen asleep.

***

A clammy finger prodded my left cheek. I opened my eyes to see my sister's round face, dewy with sweat, directly above me.

"I need to pee," she whispered in a pained voice.

I groaned. "Okay." When I sat up, my head felt like it was splitting in two. The migraine had intensified tenfold since I had fallen asleep.

"You okay?" Lalia asked, looking up at me worriedly.

"Yeah," I mumbled, wincing and gripping my head as we stumbled out of the compartment.

I didn't have a watch on and I had forgotten to look at my phone before exiting, but it must've been late because Dafne breathed heavily in the compartment next to us, and on the opposite side my grandfather snored.

As I stepped outside onto the sand, my head felt so faint I could hardly walk. I made it as far as the bonfire—which was still crackling with a few people sitting around it—before I had to stop and kneel on the sand.

"River!" Lalia squealed.

"I'm okay, I just have a really bad headache."

"Are you all right?" Hassan called from the fire.

I looked up, squinting and trying to see through the pain. He approached and bent down, touching my shoulder.

"I have a bad migraine," I managed.

"Then what are you doing out here?" he asked. "Go

back to bed."

"My sister needs the toilet."

"I'll take her to the ladies' and wait outside for her. You stay here."

"Thanks," I said, looking at him gratefully.

He took Lalia's hand and began leading her across the dunes toward the ladies' caravan. The path was lit by dozens of solar flashlights dug into the sand to form a pathway from the tents to the toilets. They reached the caravan. Lalia climbed up the steps while Hassan waited. I could see that he had turned to face me.

I tried sitting cross-legged. Slowly, I was feeling less faint, although my head still hurt like it'd been hit with a hammer. I must've spent way too long in the heat. Even though I'd worn a thick headscarf, I just wasn't used to this harsh climate.

I looked over at the bonfire. Hassan's father still sat by it with a few other diggers I had exchanged a few words with earlier. Back at the ladies' toilet, I was relieved to see Lalia had exited and begun descending the steps. She reached for Hassan's hand and they began walking back toward us.

I had to make it back to the tent. Fixing my eyes on my feet, I stood up slowly so that the blood wouldn't rush too quickly from my head.

A yell and a scream pierced the night air.

My gaze shot back toward the direction of the toilets.

Shock paralyzed my body as a dark figure collided with Hassan and my sister. It was moving so fast, I could barely even make out what it was. It lifted them both off their feet and dragged them away so fast that after a few seconds their screams had faded into the distance.

I thought standing up again must have caused me to hallucinate, but when I looked back toward the spot where they had been standing, they were gone.

Chapter 5: River

My throat was so tight with terror, I couldn't even scream.

"Help," I choked, staring in the direction my sister and Hassan had disappeared. I staggered toward the bonfire. "Help!"

Yusuf was already racing over along with a dozen other men. "Who was screaming? What happened?" he asked, panic in his eyes.

"My sister! Hassan! Someone just took them!" I pointed with a trembling hand. I began racing forward.

"Who?" Yusuf shouted.

"I don't know! They went in that direction!"

"Someone get a truck!" Yusuf bellowed.

Even as I continued running, several trucks started up and growled, and then one approached behind me. I leapt into the passenger's seat as it was moving to find Fariss in the driver's seat.

"Faster!" I urged.

I kept scanning the area, but I could see nothing but empty desert. I couldn't hear even the faintest scream.

"Lalia!" I screamed out until my lungs felt bruised. We continued to race forward in the truck along with several others who had joined us. We drove further and further into the desert. When Fariss began slowing, I turned on him.

"Why are you stopping?"

"We need to contact the police," he said.

"But they'll come too late! Keep going!"

I was close to shoving him out of the truck and taking the wheel myself when my grandfather called out to my right. He was sitting in the driver's seat of another truck next to Yusuf, both looking as terrified as

I felt.

"What exactly did you see?" my grandfather demanded.

"We don't have time to talk! We need to find them!"

"We need to call the police," Yusuf said, leaping from the van and walking over to me. He gripped my shoulders through the window. "What happened exactly?"

"My sister… She needed to use the toilet. I wasn't feeling well. Hassan waited outside for her. Once she finished, they both started walking toward me. Then someone… s-something just crashed into them and dragged them off. They disappeared so fast, I didn't even have time to scream."

I felt crazy even as I replayed the vision in my mind. It was like someone had sped by on a motorcycle, the fastest to ever be invented, and kidnapped them. But I'd heard no sound. And who the hell would want to kidnap Hassan or my sister?

Tears spilled from my eyes.

Where has my sister been taken?

She has asthma. What if she has an attack?

I turned back to Fariss. "Please! Keep going!"

The blood drained from Yusuf's face. "We need to contact the police right away. They can send helicopters. In the meantime, four trucks should continue searching." He turned to my grandfather. "Samir, return immediately to the city. Contact the police as soon as you can get a signal. River, you should go with him."

"No. I can't. I'm staying to search."

He didn't try to convince me otherwise and I was grateful for it. He got in the car that I was in, and my grandfather hurried back to the other one and headed back. *Keep Dafne safe, Grandpa.*

We remained with the other four cars who'd accompanied us out here.

I brushed away the tears furiously and fixed my gaze straight ahead.

We fell into tense silence as the four trucks, their headlights on full blast, roared over the sand dunes. I lost track of how much time we traveled—it must've been hours. But we still had not spotted even the slightest clue as to where Lalia and Hassan were.

Finally, our vehicle pulled to a stop again.

"We're going to run out of fuel if we don't return," Fariss said, eyeing the gauge.

"Then you return and we'll continue in one of the others," I said, already opening the door and stepping out.

To my horror, none of the other vehicles had much fuel left either. And we had to keep enough for the journey back.

I would have continued barefoot with my flashlight if it meant finding my sister, but Yusuf pulled me back in the vehicle.

"We need to return, River," he said, his voice weak. "We simply can't go any further or we'll all be stuck out here. We have to rally the police."

My stomach clenched as the vehicles began roaring in the opposite direction, back toward the camp, away from my sister.

I could barely see as my eyes blurred again. I wasn't even aware of my migraine anymore. The agony in my chest had crushed it into insignificance.

"The army?" Fariss said abruptly, pointing toward

our right. I wiped my eyes and stared out of the window to see a cluster of tanks.

"Stop the car!" I said instantly.

I recognized those tanks. They looked like the same ones we'd seen the day before near the restaurant.

"Wait here for me," I said.

"What? River, where—"

I didn't give Yusuf a chance to finish his question. I slammed the car door shut and began racing full speed toward the tanks.

The harsh grains of sand had now seeped into my shoes and were grating against the soles of my feet, but I barely felt the pain. My eyes were fixed on the dark machines.

As I reached the first one, there was nobody in sight. I banged against one of the walls and shouted.

"Open up! Please! It's an emergency!"

Silence.

I moved to the next one and banged again.

"Please!" I cried, even as my voice cracked.

My heart lifted as several hatches clicked open at once. Four men raised their heads out and looked down at me.

"Please! I need your help! My sister and a young man just went missing. We are camping some miles away, and someone just came by and took them. Have you seen anything at all?"

A man with short cropped hair and a scar across his right cheek climbed out and dropped down on the ground, the three other men following after him. He approached me, looking down at me seriously.

"Tell me, what exactly did you see?"

I took a deep breath and tried to steady my nerves to best express what had happened.

I repeated the incident and once again felt crazy as I recalled the speed of whomever it was who'd taken them.

They were silent as I finished, but the glances they exchanged with each other made me believe that they knew something.

"So have you seen anything?" I asked, daring to raise my hopes. "Do you have any idea at all what happened?"

There was a long pause. Then the man with the scar

cleared his throat and said, "I'm sorry. We can't help."

My heart sank into my stomach. From the way he'd listened, and the look in their eyes, I was certain that they knew something.

"Sir, you may not be able to help, but please, tell me what you know. It's my sister... my little—" My voice broke. "Why are you all here in the first place?" I managed. "What are you waiting for?"

The men began backing away. "I'm sorry," the man repeated.

I lurched forward and grabbed the man's arm. "Please!"

He brushed me off and Yusuf—who'd followed after me—grabbed my arm and pulled me back.

"River, these men don't know anything. The best thing we can do now is return and give a full account to the police."

I looked back at the men closing their hatches. They knew more than they were letting on. I just knew it.

Still, they were refusing to speak to me anymore and Yusuf was tugging me back toward the car. I had no choice but to retreat, so we sped back across the desert toward the city. We didn't even stop at camp as we reached it—we passed right by.

About two hours into the journey, we were afraid that we might run out of fuel completely—we'd done a lot of extra driving that had not been planned for. But by some mercy we managed to arrive at the borders of the city and reach a fuel station before the engine became completely empty.

Fariss got out of the car with Yusuf to refuel. When they returned, we headed straight for the nearest police station.

We hurried into the reception area that was filled with a surprisingly large crowd of people.

"I have an emergency!" Yusuf shouted in Arabic, cutting through the noise.

A policewoman approached. "What is it?" she asked.

"A seventeen-year-old boy and a six-year-old girl went missing in the desert late last night. Has a man called Samir Haik arrived here?"

Recognition spread across her face. "Yes, come with me. You are witnesses?"

Yusuf gestured to me. "She is a witness."

She led me and Yusuf along a winding corridor. We reached an office and stepped inside. There we found my grandfather and Dafne seated in front of a desk. My sister's eyes were bloodshot, and she looked terrified. My grandfather looked relieved to see us.

The woman took a seat behind the desk next to a policeman who was already sitting there.

"We have a witness," she said, pointing to me.

"Well? What can you tell us?" the policeman asked.

I could understand Arabic, but I couldn't speak it as well. I wasn't about to take chances on his English though, so I recounted the whole incident again in Arabic as well as I could.

"Have search parties been sent out already?" I asked.

The policeman and my grandfather nodded. "But anything more we can add to this case will help, of course," the policeman replied.

"Have they sent helicopters?" Yusuf asked.

"They're on their way," the policewoman replied.

"Are you aware of a group of Americans in the desert with tanks? Do they have permission to be there? What are they doing?" I asked.

The policeman and woman eyed each other, then shrugged. "We are not aware of them. But I will verify their authorization to be here."

We remained sitting in that office throughout the early hours of the morning. Officers came in and out, and we listened to reports of progress. I held my hands clasped together, praying every time a speaker crackled or an officer came in that they would have found them.

But 11am came around and they still hadn't located either Lalia or Hassan.

"At least now that it's daytime, we can see more easily," the policeman said, rubbing his eyes wearily.

I looked toward my grandfather and Dafne. She had fallen asleep against his chest.

"Let's return home for a short rest," my grandfather said. "Sitting here any longer is not going to help. We've told the police all we know. We can return again this afternoon."

Although I knew what he was saying made sense, leaving the police station felt like yet another step away from my sister. Still, Yusuf and I agreed and we headed to the car. Fariss drove us back to my grandfather's home.

There was no way I could sleep no matter how tired I was. Clearly neither could Yusuf. He retreated into the living room and began making phone calls—presumably to his wife and relatives.

My grandfather carried Dafne upstairs to her bedroom. I found myself standing in the hallway with Fariss, who looked exhausted.

I still couldn't get those strange American soldiers out of my mind. What were they doing in that part of the desert, so close to where my sister and Hassan had disappeared? I just knew that they had some clue about what had happened. I couldn't shake the feeling.

Fariss was about to return to the car, presumably to drive home for a sleep, but something made me call out and stop him.

"Fariss, would you do something for me?"

"What would that be, Miss Giovanni?"

"I need you to take me back to that area where we saw those tanks," I said.

He looked nervously at me and I was sure that he was about to refuse.

"Please," I begged before he could object. "I will talk to my grandfather and convince him to let us go."

He rubbed his forehead. "All right, I will take you there. But I really need to sleep, otherwise I'm sure I will crash before we ever reach the desert."

"Okay," I said. I understood he must've been exhausted, but I couldn't help but feel frustrated all the same. "How much time do you need?"

"Give me four hours."

"Then can you sleep in one of the spare rooms here? Traveling back to your home will just waste time."

"Okay," he said.

I took him up the stairs and showed him one of the spare bedrooms. I met my grandfather on the staircase on my way back down to the ground floor.

"Fariss is sleeping in one of the bedrooms," I said. "He agreed to take me back to the desert, to where we saw those tanks."

My grandfather stared at me. "I don't understand what good returning there will do. Yusuf said that you already asked them and they had no idea about the situation."

"I just don't believe them," I said. "I want to return there with Fariss to watch them for a few hours. Perhaps overnight."

"I don't like the idea of you two going alone. If you insist on going, I'll come with you."

"No, Grandpa. You should stay. Dafne needs someone from her family here. If you want to send another person with me, then ask Bashira if she will come."

He sighed, then nodded. "Let's ask Bashira."

We headed to the kitchen where she was seated, looking pale and sipping from a cup of tea. We explained the plan and she agreed with little hesitation. So it was decided. Once Fariss finished sleeping, we would head back to the desert.

The next four hours were possibly the hardest of my life. They felt like an eternity. I tried to find things to do around the house—like search for a flashlight to pack in my travel backpack and take a shower—but nothing made the time pass any more quickly. My grandfather suggested calling my mother, but I refused. I kept telling myself that we would find Lalia soon.

That there was no need to worry my mother. We'd tell her the story once Lalia was safe at home again. I had to keep thinking like this, otherwise I would sink into a pit of despair. I had to stay strong. We all had to.

Finally the staircase creaked and Fariss descended it. He looked refreshed. He looked from me to my grandfather. "Will you be coming, sir?" he asked.

My grandfather shook his head. "Bashira and River will be going with you."

"Very well," he said.

In the meantime, Bashira had been preparing lots of food and water to take with us in case something happened and we got stuck out in the desert longer than we had expected. I wanted to stay at least the whole night in the desert, camp out in the car and keep an eye on the Americans to see what they were doing—assuming they were even still there.

I gave my grandfather a hug. Then we exited the house and climbed back into the white truck.

We sped up along the road, and although the tank was nearly full, we stopped by a gas station and filled it right up. We also stocked up on some extra fuel just in case we ran out.

And then we headed straight for the desert. We barely talked as we traveled beneath the late-afternoon sun. I just kept looking straight ahead through the windshield. About halfway, exhaustion caught up with me. My eyelids began to droop. I figured it was better to take a nap now than tonight when I needed to be alert and watching. I drifted in and out of sleep for the rest of the journey.

"Over there," Fariss said, pointing to a cluster of tanks in the distance. I was relieved that they were still here.

"Good," I said, leaning forward in my seat. "We should try to remain hidden from them. I don't want them to know that we're spying on them." We had stopped on a raised mound of sand that sloped downward toward the area where the tanks were stationed. This gave us a good view of their camp. But we were too exposed for my liking. Fariss pulled back a little so that we were a bit less visible but could still see everything that was going on.

And then the wait began. Once the sun had set

behind the horizon, men began to climb out of the tanks and stretch their legs. I rummaged in the front compartment of the vehicle and found a pair of binoculars. I looked through them and zoomed in to get a better look.

They all seemed to wear belts with the same equipment I'd seen the two men wearing the other night—sharp wooden spears, silver guns, and boxlike objects with flashing lights. I also noticed some other odd-looking technology that I couldn't put a name to. Some of them sat on top of the tanks, looking north, while others walked around the area or leaned against the tanks, eating and talking.

What I wouldn't give to overhear their conversations.

I looked at Fariss, then at Bashira—who was beginning to nod off in the backseat of the car.

"I need to hear what they're saying," I whispered.

"Miss Giovanni," Fariss said, looking nervous, "you didn't say that you would want to leave the truck."

"I promise I'll be fine, I just need to do this."

I grabbed my backpack and a bottle of water, opened the door and stepped out onto the ground.

"Miss Giovanni," Fariss called, "don't go too far. And watch out for dangerous creatures—cobras and scorpions in particular."

I gulped. "Thanks." I put the bottle of water into my backpack and then pulled out the flashlight, tucked it into my belt and flung the bag back over my shoulders. Then I positioned the hood of my dark-colored jacket so that it covered my face as much as possible.

I began making my way down the slope. Of course I couldn't use my flashlight or I would attract their attention. That was just in case of an emergency. I had to go by the light of the moon and stars.

When I was level with the tanks, I could already hear better. I was just about close enough to begin making sense of their words when two men turned toward me. I dropped to the ground, hoping that they hadn't noticed. And that I hadn't just dropped down near some kind of deadly creature.

I remained still for several moments, turning my head to look toward them from my position against the ground. Although two men were still looking in my direction, it seemed that they either hadn't noticed me, or just weren't interested. They turned their backs and headed back toward the rest of the crowd.

I breathed a little more easily. Raising my head higher, I stood up slowly.

I began to move closer, but to my dismay, the conversation had died down by the time I was close enough to hear. Most of them were now staring northward in silence, guns in their hands and those odd red flashing boxes scattered around the area. I looked north myself, trying to understand what they were all staring at. I couldn't see anything but endless sand dunes.

What are they all waiting for?

I decided to start walking in the direction where they were staring. I kept down low against the ground, careful to keep an eye out for creepy-crawlies. I had to catch my scream in my throat as a hideous black scorpion scuttled out from a hole in the sand about a foot away. It nearly crawled over my feet.

After that, I remained standing, praying that I wouldn't encounter another dangerous creature before

I returned to the truck.

I swerved out wider, further away from the men to avoid being seen, and continued walking north, looking back every now and then to be sure nobody had noticed me.

I was about to see the futility of my attempt and return to the vehicle when a sharp pain filled my skull. It felt like I'd just walked headfirst into a wall. I staggered back, cursing and clutching my forehead.

What in the world…?

Reaching out a hand, I was shocked to find something hard.

I've got to be hallucinating.

I stretched out my other hand. That also touched something hard. It was the most bizarre thing I'd ever experienced in my life, like some kind of invisible barrier. I moved my hands along the hard surface. It felt neither rough nor smooth… I didn't even know how to describe its texture, if it even had a texture. It just hurt like hell to walk into.

Blinking hard, I looked toward the truck still parked up on the mound of sand. Then I looked back at the tanks. I didn't think that I was hallucinating.

What is this? I walked further, keeping my hands against this strange invisible force field. After twenty minutes of walking, I was about to run back to the car to get Fariss and ask what he thought when I heard a voice. A male voice, speaking English.

"No, Marilyn."

It sounded like it was coming from behind the barrier and yet, when I looked straight through it, I saw nothing but sand. *Where is it coming from?* It sounded so close.

Then there was a wailing—presumably a female's.

The male voice spoke again. "Why don't you go and spend the night with your boyfriend for a change?"

"Because he's not mine anymore! He's got a new girlfriend!" She sounded hysterical.

Where on earth are these people? I found myself looking in all directions, even down at the ground, wondering if there was some kind of bunker beneath me. No. It was coming from behind this strange invisible wall.

Clenching my fists, I called out, "Who are you?"

The man and woman fell silent.

Rapid footsteps crossed the sand, and then I heard deep breathing only feet away from me. My heart hammered against my chest. I felt a presence so close to me, and yet I still couldn't see anyone.

Could they be... ghosts?

I shook myself.

Don't be so stupid.

Ghosts don't exist.

"What brings a young woman like you out here so late?" The male spoke.

I shuddered at the proximity of his voice.

"I'm looking for my sister," I replied, even as I felt crazy for talking to thin air. "A six-year-old girl. She went missing about twenty-four hours ago. She's plump, has brown hair, turquoise eyes and light tan skin. H-Have you—?"

Before I could finish my question, a cold hand shot out from nowhere and gripped my wrist. Next thing I knew, I was being pulled through what had previously been an impenetrable barrier. I landed on the ground near a pair of large feet. Shock coursing through my veins, I raised my eyes to see a tall, blond-haired, brown-eyed young man standing over me. He was terribly pale and there was a strange vibrancy to his irises, almost as though he were wearing special contact lenses.

"Yes," he responded calmly, his gaze roaming the length of my body. "We have your sister. And now we have you."

Chapter 6: River

I screamed as the man bent down and gripped my neck with his freezing hands. His grip was so strong, he could crush my windpipe with the slightest bit of pressure.

He raised me to my feet and stared down at me.

"Who are you?" I choked.

He ignored me and looked over at a blonde woman standing next to him. She also looked unnaturally pale. I strained to see where I'd just been pulled through. I was able to spot the white truck in the distance.

"Help!" I shouted.

"That's it," the man said softly, looking up toward where I was looking. "Call for help. See what good it does you."

To my surprise, he let go of me. I made a dash toward the vehicle but smashed into the barrier again, the same barrier I'd just been pulled through. I continued yelling for help.

The truck's engine roared in the distance and it began trundling down the sand dunes toward us, headlights on full blast. It approached near where I was standing, then drove right past. I could see Bashira and Fariss looking around in bewilderment.

They can't see me.

I whirled around to see the man watching me with almost boredom.

"What's your name?" he asked.

Ripping out the flashlight that was still stuffed in my belt, I hurled it at his face and darted in the opposite direction. Even though I couldn't pass through the barrier, that didn't stop me from trying to get as far away from this man as possible. I didn't stop to see if the flashlight had hit its mark. Whatever the case, it hadn't done enough damage because he caught up with me in a matter of seconds. He tripped me up and knocked me to the ground again.

"Come now," he said, bending down closer to me and touching my cheek with his cold fingers. "No need to get us off to such a rough start."

The blonde woman was now standing right next to us. Her eyes looked swollen from crying and black mascara stained her cheeks. "What are you going to do with this one, Michael?" she asked.

Michael.

"I need to consult Jeramiah," he said.

Jeramiah?

I made another attempt to scramble away, but he was unnaturally fast. He'd gripped my waist before I'd even managed to stand up.

"You'll do better not to struggle," he said calmly.

Lifting me from the ground, he flung me over his shoulder. Then he lurched forward with such speed, it knocked the breath out of me. The wind whipped against my ears. It felt like I was falling, not being carried.

He stopped at a large trapdoor fixed into the sand. The blonde girl stooped and pulled it open, then Michael carried me inside. Still wrestling with me as I fought him, he descended a narrow staircase.

I gasped as we touched down on a shiny marble floor. We were standing on a platform surrounded by glass walls at the top level of a huge atrium. It had too many layers for me to count, and it was lavishly decorated, with a sprawling garden in the center and massive chandeliers hanging from the ceiling.

"Who the hell are you?" I shouted again, kicking and pounding my fists against his back. He barely seemed to notice my struggle as he headed with me toward an elevator. Marilyn entered after us and pushed a button.

"Why don't you just tell her?" the young woman said, rubbing her temples as the elevator began to descend. "Her questions are giving me a headache."

Michael shot a look at Marilyn.

"I'll tell her when I tell her," he snapped.

Marilyn crossed her arms over her chest and scowled

at Michael.

I continued to attack my captor's back—and any other part of his body I could reach—but he didn't seem to feel a thing. My attempts to break free only made his freezing hands close more tightly around my legs.

"Please," I gasped. "Please. Let me down!"

Both of them ignored me as the elevator came to a stop and the doors slid open. Marilyn took a left turn and headed in the opposite direction from Michael and me. I strained my neck to see where he was taking me as he sped up along a wide veranda. We passed closed door after closed door, his footsteps echoing off the sleek floors. Finally Michael stopped in front of one of the doors and rapped his knuckles against it.

I held my breath as there was a loud click and the door swung open. Michael's hands ran up my thighs and gripped my waist. He lowered me to the floor. I tried to dart away from him, back out of the door, but he held me firmly in place—my back against his chest, forcing me to face forward.

My eyes fell on the man standing before me in the

hallway of a luxurious apartment. He was tall, even taller than Michael. He had a robe draped around his broad shoulders, partially revealing a chiseled torso. He had dark shoulder-length hair and harsh blue eyes that roamed me curiously.

"Who's this?" he asked, his voice low and deep.

"Jeramiah, she walked right up to us. I couldn't resist…"

I flinched as the blue-eyed man stepped forward and placed a hand beneath my chin, tilting my head upward. Then he let go and lowered his face to my neck before breathing in.

"Hmm," Jeramiah murmured. "Take her down to the basement."

I felt the blood drain from my face.

I was still holding out hope that this was all just a dream. I must've fallen asleep in the car on the way to the tanks. The trauma of losing my sister had brought about this crazy nightmare I couldn't escape from…

Jeramiah took a step backward and a beautiful ebony-skinned girl appeared by his side. Dressed in a short nightdress, she wrapped her arms around his waist and settled her gaze on me.

"The basement?" she asked, her voice silvery. "Really, Jeramiah? She's a beauty."

Jeramiah heaved a sigh and studied me again.

"She is a beauty," he said thoughtfully, after a pause.

"I was going to suggest that I keep her," Michael said.

Keep me?

"Please!" I stammered. "Where's my sister?"

Jeramiah raised a dark brow, then spoke as if he hadn't heard me. "After the kidnappings this week, we've already selected enough humans to half-turn. Keeping her in the upper levels would upset the ratio," he said.

Half-turn?

Ratio?

What is he talking about?

There was a pause. "I could... restore it," Michael said.

"You know I don't like waste, Michael," Jeramiah replied, his eyes stern.

"Don't worry. I'll pick one of the servants who's

been slacking recently… I already have one in mind. Leave it to me."

Jeramiah still looked doubtful. "When will you do it?"

"By the end of the week," Michael replied.

"No later than that."

"Agreed," Michael said.

"But Michael," the beauty standing next to Jeramiah said, "I was thinking this newcomer could be good for our new member, Joseph. What about you and Alexandria?"

Michael breathed out impatiently and gripped my arms tighter. "Alexandria and I are tired of each other. And as much as I appreciate your opinion, Lucretia, it isn't required. Joseph isn't interested in a companion anyway, according to Jeramiah… So this girl has arrived just in time. We were planning to do it this evening, right?"

Jeramiah's eyes were still fixed on me, but he nodded. "Yes, this evening."

"What is this evening?" I asked, hysteria shaking my voice.

Again, nobody bothered to answer me.

"Have you been to see Joseph?" Michael asked.

"No. I'm going to do that now," Jeramiah replied.

"Are we sure that he's ready for it?" Michael asked. "He seemed… unsteady."

"I think he's ready. We'll have him see people one by one, so it won't be so overwhelming. I'll stay with him in case there is any trouble."

"He'd better be ready," Michael muttered. "He won't be newly-turned for much longer…"

Michael moved back down the hallway toward the door, dragging me after him.

"I'll bring Joseph to your quarters, yes?" Jeramiah said, already pulling on a shirt that his girlfriend was handing him.

"Yes," Michael said. "We're headed there now."

"We might as well bring him to see this girl first then," Jeramiah said.

"I agree," Michael replied.

"Who's Joseph?" I shouted.

Michael threw me over his shoulder again and left the apartment. He ran along the veranda outside so fast

I could hardly breathe. My surroundings were a blur. I could barely even open my eyes until he stopped outside another door.

"My sister. She's not well. She has asthma. At least take me to see her!"

"Don't worry about your sister," he replied calmly. "She's in capable hands."

Whose hands?

Withdrawing a key from his pocket, he opened the door and stepped inside. I shivered as he locked it behind him. We were standing in another apartment that looked similar in luxury to Jeramiah's. He carried me down the hallway, pushed open the door at the end of it, and stepped into a bedroom. He placed me down on the large circular bed in the center of the room.

As soon as I hit the mattress, I scrambled away from him and ran for the door. He whizzed across the room and shut it before I could reach it. I staggered backward, moving toward the far corner of the room and looking for anything that I could use to defend myself.

"What are you?" I breathed.

A smile curled his lips, his brown eyes fixed on my face.

"Come here and I'll show you."

I grabbed hold of a table lamp and pulled it from its socket, brandishing it to create as much distance between him and me as I could.

Calmly, he removed his jacket to reveal a thin shirt beneath it. He walked toward me slowly, like a lion stalking its prey. Then his arm shot out so fast I didn't have the speed to react in time. He ripped the lamp from my hands and threw it out of reach. Now defenseless, I stood flush against the wall.

"Do as I say, and you have nothing to be afraid of."

As he took his final step, his body pressed against me, pinning me to the wall. He gripped the collar of my shirt and ripped it downward, baring my neck and collarbone.

"No!" I screamed, clutching my ripped shirt with one hand while trying to push him away with the other.

He pinned my hands up against the wall and held them there, then lowered his head to my neck. I tensed up as his lips pressed against my skin. I thought he was kissing me at first, then two sharp stabs punctured my flesh. I was too shocked to even scream.

What is happening?

His tongue brushed my skin, and he began sucking. He groaned deeply, and I felt his entire body begin heaving against me.

He's... drinking my blood?

I felt close to passing out as he continued to take deep gulps of me.

Wake up, River. Please... wake up.

When he finally raised his head, my head was faint. His lips were covered with deep red liquid. My own blood. He smiled, revealing sharp fangs.

"Do I still need to answer your question, treasure? Or have I shown you enough?"

He had shown me enough.

These people were vampires.

Chapter 7: Ben

I'd been trying to keep my head down as much as possible. Jeramiah had consulted with Michael and Amaya, and he'd given me a few other jobs—mostly menial tasks like tending to the lily pond. I did them dutifully. My plan was to do as I was requested until I felt the time was right to propose that I accompany them on one of their hunts.

I had to gain their trust first. It seemed like the most obvious thing that a vampire would ask if he wanted to escape—to accompany them beyond the boundary. I needed to be patient and show Jeramiah that I was committed to being a good citizen of The Oasis.

I was invited to join more parties at night, but I declined. I just told them I was a recluse and had never been one to party. Nobody seemed to raise much objection to it. Marilyn didn't bother me again either. Nobody other than Jeramiah sought me out, and even then just when there was a specific task he wanted to talk to me about, or to deliver more blood. There never seemed to be any shortage of it—indeed, he encouraged me to drink as much as I wanted. Though I didn't, of course. I just drank the minimum required to survive without climbing the walls from hunger. I was just grateful that I hadn't needed to do any killing myself. The moment I did that again, I'd be plunged back into the same black state I'd been in while drifting in the submarine.

When there was a knock on my door in the early hours of the night, I assumed it would be Jeramiah. I was right.

"Jeramiah," I said.

"Would you come with me?" he said.

"What is it?"

"It's easier if I just show you."

"All right." I wasn't wearing a shirt, but I just went with him as I was. I doubted he'd keep me long, whatever it was.

He was silent as we walked along the veranda. He stopped eventually outside the door of an apartment.

He knocked on the door. "Michael," he called.

So this is Michael's apartment. I wondered why he was bringing me here of all places.

There were footsteps and the door opened. Michael appeared behind it, his lower lip stained with blood. Perhaps we'd interrupted him during a meal. The traces of human blood on his mouth made my stomach lurch, even though I had already downed three glasses earlier this evening.

"Come in," Michael said—more to Jeramiah than to me. He opened the door wider and stepped aside as we entered.

I still didn't understand what Michael found so objectionable about me—I'd never done anything to insult or harm him. Not that I gave a damn.

"Through here," Michael said, leading us along the long corridor. He took a left down another hallway and stopped outside a door at the end of it. He drew out a small key from his pocket and opened it. Before I even realized what was happening, Jeramiah had stepped behind me and pushed me through the door into what turned out to be an unheated sauna room. Following closely behind me, he slammed the door shut after us.

I was confused at first as to Jeramiah's hurry to get me in the room, but then I was aware of nothing but the scent of hot human blood overwhelming me. As I laid eyes on a young woman cowering in one corner of the paneled room, puncture wounds in her neck still bleeding, I realized that agreeing to come here with Jeramiah had been a terrible, terrible mistake.

CHAPTER 8: RIVER

My head was still spinning.

Vampires.

They exist.

Did this mean that other creatures my mother and I had seen reported on TV existed too? Witches? Dragons?

I felt like I'd gone insane even entertaining the thought.

And yet here I was locked in this sauna room with fang marks in my neck.

I was past hoping that I would wake up.

This was no dream.

When the door opened, I was terrified that it would be Michael back for more of my blood. The sight I was met with was no less terrifying: two vampires—Jeramiah, and another young man who looked over six feet tall, with deep green eyes and dark, almost black hair.

My first thought was that this must be the Joseph person Jeramiah and Michael had been talking about earlier.

Now I wondered whether it would have been better for me if Michael had shown up again.

I was expecting one of them, perhaps both of them, to launch on me and inflict more pain, perhaps even end my life. Instead, the green-eyed man jerked backward the moment he laid eyes on me and darted toward the door. Jeramiah reached it before him and blocked his exit. Joseph's shoulders were heaving as he kept his back facing me.

"What's wrong?" Jeramiah asked.

"I'm willing to serve The Oasis, but not like this,"

Joseph said, his voice deep and strained.

"I'm not going to ask you to kill this girl. Just half-turn her."

"Step aside." There was urgency in Joseph's tone.

"You said that you felt you were ready to come out with us on a hunt," Jeramiah continued, making no motion to step out of the way. "Half-turning humans shouldn't be difficult. And I'm here to oversee it. I'll make sure you don't take things too far—"

Joseph gripped Jeramiah's shoulder and shoved him aside. Casting him a glare, he said through gritted teeth, "I can't... touch this girl."

He clutched the handle, forced the door open and stormed out of the room.

I wasn't sure whether to be relieved or dread what was to happen next.

My stomach squirmed as Michael stepped back into the room with Jeramiah.

"Now what?" Michael said, eyeing me.

Jeramiah looked quite unfazed. "Joseph isn't going to do it," he replied. "So that means we're going to have to create another new vampire from one of our humans."

"Which one?"

"It doesn't matter much," Jeramiah said. "Just choose one who is smaller than us—someone who won't be impossible to control soon after their turning. Because I'm not willing to wait days for a new vampire to calm down. As soon as they turn, they'll begin work right away."

"A damn annoyance only new vampires can half-turn humans," Michael muttered.

Both men stepped out of the room. The door shut behind them, leaving me alone.

It was all I could do to not lose myself to despair when I imagined what my sister might be going through. I could only pray that she was being treated better than me. *But what do they want her for? What do they want me for?*

My chest ached as I imagined how sweet Lalia's blood might taste to them.

Please, Laly, wherever you are, be safe. I'm here. I'm gonna come for you as soon as I can.

I almost leapt out of my skin as the door swung

open again. It was Jeramiah, alone this time. He was holding a syringe. Panicking, I scrambled to my feet and tried to distance myself from him, but he closed in on me.

"Be still," he said calmly as he slid a hand around the back of my neck and positioned me against the wall. I struggled until the needle pricked my skin and the drug seeped into my bloodstream. Consciousness soon left me after that. The numbness was an unexpected mercy.

Chapter 9: Ben

I was fuming as I returned to my apartment. I shouldn't have been surprised that the day had come when Jeramiah expected me to half-turn humans. After all, Jeramiah had said all along that was what I was useful for—but I couldn't help but feel furious at the way he'd sprung it on me. The fact that he hadn't told me what he'd come for when he'd first knocked on my door made me believe that he'd thought that I would disagree.

As much as I knew this would set me back in my

attempt to gain the vampires' trust and escape this place, I simply couldn't bring myself to bite into that innocent girl's flesh. I knew that the moment I held her in my arms, I would lose myself in her and resurface again only to find her a shriveled corpse.

Jeramiah didn't know who I was. He thought that he would be strong enough to control me. Although he was a Novak himself, I doubted that there was anyone who could restrain me when I was in the midst of a blood frenzy. Even my father had trouble controlling me back in The Shade.

There was something very wrong with me, and until I found out what it was, I couldn't risk killing again.

My mouth watered as I recalled that human girl huddled in the corner of the sauna. When Jeramiah had closed the door, I had been so sure that I would launch at her and rip her throat out. If I had not shoved him aside, I would've drained every last drop from her.

My breathing was heavy as I recalled the scent of her blood and I felt a burning hunger in my stomach. Before Jeramiah had knocked on my door, I had been satisfied. Now, I was craving blood again.

I headed straight for the kitchen and opened the fridge door. I pulled out every single jug of blood that was stored there except for one. I drank it all, and as I finished the last gulp, even that didn't satisfy me. Having a human so close to me had reignited the darkness that lingered beneath the surface.

I gripped the table hard.

This was the most human blood I'd consumed since I had last murdered, before arriving in The Oasis. I had been so careful to consume only as much as my body absolutely needed. Now it seemed that I needed so much more just to keep my craving in check. Just looking at that human had set me back so far.

If this was how I still acted around humans, what was I going to do once I managed to escape this place? I knew that I had to escape, but I still didn't know how I would cope without murdering every human who had the misfortune of crossing paths with me.

Dammit. Why can't I just drink animal blood like the rest of my family?

As I stood in the kitchen, it occurred to me that it

had actually been some time now since I had last tried to drink animal blood. Perhaps something in my body had settled down by now and I could handle it. I found it hard to believe, but there was only one way to know for sure.

Walking to my bedroom, I pulled on a shirt. Then I left my apartment and descended to the bottom level of the atrium. I walked through the gardens, scanning the rooms that surrounded it. I looked for the one where I had seen the vampire retreat with the snake that had recently escaped. I was not sure if there were other animals in The Oasis, but snake blood should be good enough to test my theory.

Once I thought that I had spotted the right room, I left the gardens and approached it. I gripped the handle of the door and was pleased to see that it was open. I found myself stepping into a large room filled with cages of writhing snakes of all shapes and sizes.

Why do they keep all of these snakes?

I had gotten the impression that the vampires here only drank human blood. Why would they drink anything else when they had so much of it, and of such quality?

Whatever reason they had for keeping them, it suited me right now. I approached the cage nearest to me and scanned the snakes inside it, wondering which to pull out. Then I noticed the huge black snake that had tried to attack me out in the gardens in the next cage and decided he—or she—would be a worthy target.

When I opened the cage, the black snake darted towards me, its fangs bared. I caught it by its neck and squeezed hard before it could bite me, then jerked it upward, pulling the rest of its tail out of the cage. I closed the cage again before any other snakes could attempt an escape.

The black snake's tail thrashed about as it continued trying to attack me. I didn't prolong its death. Drawing out my claws, I sliced off its head in one swift motion. As blood began to spill from its body, even just the smell of it made my stomach lurch. It was hard to describe the smell. It was just foul. Something I would never want to put in my mouth.

Still, I forced myself to dig my fangs into its flesh

and draw a long deep gulp.

I held my nose as I swallowed, then waited.

After twenty seconds, nothing had happened, so I took another deep gulp. And then another. That was about all I could handle of the vile substance in one go, so I set the body down on the ground and sat down on a bench in one corner of the room. I still held my nose even now, afraid that if I stopped, I would upchuck everything.

After two minutes, a wave of relief washed over me. *Animal blood still tastes disgusting, but perhaps I can stomach it now. Maybe I really have changed. Maybe all I needed was some time to settle into this new body.*

I was starting to feel so confident that I got up for another gulp of snake blood, but as I motioned to pick up the body, my stomach growled and before I knew it, I was staring at a pool of red vomit on the floor.

I kept vomiting until it felt like if I vomited anymore, I would start throwing up my insides.

Great.

Nothing has changed.

Something is very, very wrong with me.

I looked around the room and spotted some cleaning equipment. Filling up a bucket, I grabbed a mop and cleaned up my mess. Then I picked up the corpse of the snake and left the room. I wasn't sure whether somebody would be irritated with me that I had just killed one of their snakes, or whether they wouldn't mind. They seemed to have so many, after all.

Still, I wanted to avoid trouble, so I made my way to one of the orchards that was overgrown with shrubbery. I dropped the body of the snake beneath bushes and covered it with soil. It would decompose soon enough.

Then I walked past the lily ponds and rinsed my mouth and hands in the clear water. When I stood up, my gaze landed on the memorial stone of Lucas Novak. It seemed to have been attended to since I had last laid eyes on it. It was cleaner, and I could make out the inscription better. Feeling unsettled, reminded of the urgency of escaping this place, I headed straight back to my apartment.

I could still taste snake blood on my tongue. I

walked back into the kitchen intending to finish off the last jug of blood to get rid of the taste, but when I opened the fridge, the shelves were filled with jug upon jug of delicious human blood.

Strange.

I wondered who had done it. I had only been gone a few minutes. It was almost like there was some slave living with me, watching my every move.

Although I was immensely grateful to not have to worry about finding my own blood, I couldn't help but feel that with each gulp of this exquisite blood, I was becoming more and more indebted to this strange place known as The Oasis.

CHAPTER 10: RIVER

I woke up to a burning sensation in my right upper arm. The pain was blinding. I gripped my shoulder to soothe it, but it only intensified the pain.

I sat up slowly, wincing as I opened my eyes. To my horror, I found myself in Michael's large circular bed. My heart hammered as I scanned the room, but I found some relief in the fact that he wasn't here with me. I was also still wearing my own clothes, which gave me some comfort.

I moved my ripped shirt and looked down at my

shoulder. The skin surrounding my right bicep was red and swollen, and etched into it was a black cross.

I almost yelled.

What the hell is this?

It was hurting so much, it felt like someone was still inking my skin. *What is the meaning of this cross? Why would they brand me with it?*

Although overwhelmed with doubts and questions, I didn't spend any more time staring at my arm. I was alone. Michael was nowhere in sight, nor was any other vampire. I climbed as quietly as I could out of bed.

I have to find my sister and Hassan. And we have to escape this nightmare.

The door was ajar. I was about to push it open wider and slip out when something caught my eye on the dressing table a few feet away from me. Leaving the door reluctantly, I approached it.

As I stared down at two objects wrapped in brown paper and covered with a piece of parchment, my mouth fell open and my stomach somersaulted.

A note was written in jerky black handwriting on the parchment:

"For your mother and brother."

I snatched up the note and stared at it, my hands shaking. I read the words over and over again, just in case my eyes deceived me. Then I dropped it and picked up the first object wrapped in brown paper. I tore off the paper to reveal a black silk pouch. I loosened the opening, and found myself staring down at a pile of gold coins. My heart beat faster as I reached for the second object. It was much smaller than the first, and cylindrical. I tore through the brown paper and found myself holding a thin glass vial filled with a transparent amber liquid.

What is this?

I looked around the room, breathing heavily, then back down at the objects.

How do they know about my mother and brother? What are these things for?

I jumped as a deep male voice spoke from the door.

"How are you feeling, River?" Michael asked as he stepped into the room. His blond hair looked wet, like he'd just taken a shower.

I felt all the blood drain from my face. "How do you

know my name?"

Michael's smile broadened. Reaching into his pocket, he pulled out a crumpled-up tag and placed it in my palm. I recognized it instantly as the airport label that had been on my backpack. It contained my full name… and my home address.

They know where I live.

"What are these?" I gasped, stumbling back away from him and ripping up the tag.

He eyed the gold coins and the vial. "Gifts from The Oasis."

"My mother and brother aren't here. Why would you give them these gifts?" I breathed, fearing that they were going to kidnap them too. Or had already.

Michael shook his head. "You need not worry about your family in New York. We don't go that far for humans… at least, not usually. We have plenty of healthy humans to choose from in our proximity. As to how they will receive their gifts, we will send one of our witches to deliver them. Would you like that?"

"No!" I grabbed the coins and the vial from the table and held them behind my back. "Please! Don't go near them. I'm begging you. My brother is sick—"

Michael held up a hand. "Very well. You might as well keep the gifts then. Not that they will be of much use to you around here…" He walked over to the table and opened one of the large drawers. He pulled out my backpack from it and handed it to me. I grabbed it from him and stuffed the gifts inside, then shoved the bag into one corner of the room.

"Where is my sister?" I repeated for what felt like the hundredth time.

"Your sister is fine."

"Take me to her!" I shouted.

Irritation sparked in his eyes, but I didn't hear his response as the front door to his apartment clicked open. Footsteps shuffled down the corridor, and then the bedroom door pushed wide open. Standing before me was Jeramiah, accompanied by a short woman just as deathly pale, and bound in chains. Blood was smeared around her mouth and her eyes looked unfocused as they fell on me.

I backed up against the wall, wishing there was a window in this damned place that I could leap out of.

But there were no windows anywhere here. We were underground, in the middle of a desert.

"Well, what are you waiting for?" Jeramiah said, looking at Michael. "Position her."

Before I could even attempt to get away, Michael grabbed me and wrestled me back onto the bed. He pinned me down with his knees and hands, spreading out my body so tight I couldn't even budge an inch.

The woman began to growl frighteningly, a guttural sound that came from deep within her throat. She clanked her chains and Jeramiah restrained her as they both approached the bed.

"River," Jeramiah said. It disturbed me to no end that now even he was addressing me by my name. "I would advise you not to struggle. Faye is a newly turned vampire. That means she is particularly... unpredictable. She's not as strong as me, so I can control her, but only if you cooperate. If you don't, you might find yourself bled dry. Understood?"

My eyes widened in terror as he loosened the woman's chains and she leapt on top of me. Baring her fangs, she dug them right into my neck, in a different spot where Michael had drunk from me before.

I groaned, my body stiffening as I seized up in pain.

I'd experienced needles and injections before, but these vampire teeth felt so thick compared to them, and they dug so deep into my flesh, I worried that they were going to hit bone.

I wanted to scream out, but I remembered Jeramiah's words and so I bit my lip.

"Don't suck!" Jeramiah said.

He must've done something to hurt the female vampire, because she moaned and stopped sucking so hard.

"Release now." Jeramiah spoke again.

A freezing cold substance shot into my neck. Pain lit up every nerve in my body, and all my limbs began to shake.

What is happening to me?

"Enough," Jeramiah ordered, clanking the chains, and Faye pulled away from me.

I found myself staring up at Jeramiah and Michael, who were looking down at me, but soon their faces were a blur. Everything was a blur. I could barely even form a coherent thought. All that I was aware of was the pain now coursing through my veins and the coldness, the biting coldness that seeped right through to the very marrow of my bones.

My mouth felt dry and my heart began beating so fast I thought that it would give up. It felt like my windpipe was closing and I could barely breathe.

Something touched my face—an ice-cold hand. Michael's perhaps. "You're going to be just fine, River," he said.

Cold tears streamed from my eyes as pain washed over me in waves.

I'm going to die.

I'm going to die.

And yet hours passed and I didn't. I still hung on in that strange place between consciousness and darkness.

There was no way I could have guessed how much time passed. It could have been hours or it could have been days. Moments merged into each other, passing in one long stream of pain and torment.

It was only once the trembling started to subside that I found pieces of myself again. I found it easier to think, easier to be aware of what was going on around me, and once my vision had returned, my breathing became more even.

But the coldness, the bitter coldness… it never left me. It seemed to have settled permanently in my bones. Into my very being.

I didn't understand what had just happened to me, but as strength flooded back to my limbs and I was able to sit up, one thing I knew for certain:

I was no longer the River I'd known.

CHAPTER 11: RIVER

Aside from the aching cold, my senses were surrounded by a myriad of stimuli. I could hear noises in other rooms around the atrium that I hadn't heard before, pick up on a variety of scents I hadn't detected before, and my eyesight felt ten times sharper.

I stood up from the bed and stared at myself in the mirror. My tan skin looked dull and pale. Too pale. My turquoise eyes had an odd vibrancy that hadn't been there before. I bared my teeth, fearing that I was about to see fangs… but they looked normal.

Michael got up from a chair in a shadowy corner of the room. He approached and I caught sight of him in the mirror as he placed his hands on either side of my waist.

"What am I?" I whispered, moving away from him.

"You are a half-blood… *my* half-blood."

"What is a half-blood?"

"Come with me," he said, ignoring my question. "You need to warm up. Since you're not fully a vampire, your body needs some heat or it can become very uncomfortable. You feel the cold, unlike us."

I was still in a daze. I couldn't even find it in myself to object as he took my hand and led me out of the bedroom, down the corridor toward the room he had kept me in before. The sauna. He stepped inside with me, fiddled with a panel of dials and buttons, then closed the door. The room began to heat up quickly. I stopped shivering so much, and the deep ache in my bones subsided a little.

I had so many thoughts fighting to burst out at once, I didn't know which to ask first.

"Why did you do this to me?"

"I understand that it's a shock now," he said. "But you will come to thank me for choosing you as my half-blood." He leaned in and brushed the back of his hand against my cheek. "I promise."

"*Your* half-blood?" I breathed.

"My half-blood."

I stood up and moved away from him. "What is this tattoo you placed on my arm?"

"We all have them." He rolled up his sleeve and showed me an identical brand on his right upper arm.

"Did you etch this into me?"

"That's not important. What is important is that you listen carefully to what I'm about to say. If you want to survive in this new body of yours, you'll need to learn to depend on me. I can show you how to live without pain, and how to enjoy your life."

I backed away as far as I could from him in the wooden room.

"There are certain rules," he continued, "that you are designed to abide by. My rules. If you disobey me, very bad things can end up happening to you… and your sister."

I choked up. "You have given me no proof that she's even still alive."

"I'm telling you that she is still alive. And she will remain alive and well, provided you do as I say."

"What do you want from me?"

He paused as he eyed me over. "First, I want to show you that you will enjoy having me as your master. I will be good to you and you will enjoy submitting to me."

This man is crazy.

"Come here," he said.

I didn't budge.

His eyes darkened. "Come here, River." His voice was dangerously low. "I won't ask you again."

I remained rooted to my spot.

I wasn't going to submit to this monster.

When I still didn't respond, he leapt up, grabbed my arm, and pulled me out of the sauna. He began striding down the corridor, dragging me along behind him. To my shock, I found that I could keep up without difficulty. Before, even his walking had been so fast, I could barely keep up.

He stopped at the door right at the end of the corridor, and pushed it open. It was dark but, bizarrely, I could see everything clearly. It was a small room, bare except for what looked like a huge freezer in one corner.

He moved so fast, I barely realized what happened next. He dragged me over to the container, lifted up the lid, and wrestled me inside. I submerged in icy water—so cold my body seized up. My breathing came hard and fast as the agony intensified in my bones.

"No!" I screamed.

He slammed the lid shut above me. The container was so filled up with water, even my mouth was submerged. I was forced to breathe through my nose.

I bashed against the lid, but it wouldn't budge. I kicked, and realized that I was too short to even feel the bottom. I moved my body as rapidly as I could, trying to generate warmth. I wondered whether even as a human I would feel as much pain as this. No matter how much I moved around, I was unable to conjure up even the slightest bit of heat.

I had no way of knowing the time, but it felt like an

eternity before Michael raised the lid again. My body had become so stiff I was barely able to keep myself above the surface. If he'd come even ten minutes later, I was sure that I would have drowned.

He reached inside and picked me up, and set me down roughly on the floor. Unable to stand, I collapsed.

He bent down to my level, touching my forehead with his palm.

"That was uncomfortable, wasn't it?" he asked softly.

I was in too much pain to even respond.

"River, I'm sorry. I don't like to do this to you. But you need to learn to do as I say."

He scooped me up in his arms even as I shook, and carried me out of the dark chamber. We re-emerged in the corridor and he headed back to the sauna. He set me down on one of the wooden benches and I backed up against the wall as he turned the dial up high. He didn't say a word as I sat in the corner, still trembling, until the sauna grew hot enough for the pain to begin to subside. The shock remained with me much longer, however. I was still breathing in rasps, my body still in some kind of trauma.

He reached for a towel and handed it to me.

I clasped it in my hands and buried my face in it. It was the only barrier I could form between him and me in that small room.

"Now," he said, after perhaps twenty minutes had passed. "Come here."

Even after the pain he'd put me through, I couldn't find it in myself to give in. Instead I shot him a glare. "I know your type," I spat. "Who were you before you became a vampire? Were you bullied at school? Unable to get girls based on your winning personality alone? Stay away from me, you creep."

He got to his feet slowly, and closed the distance between us. As he extended his fingers, claws shot out. He pressed his forefinger against my cheek, cutting a thin line. The blood seeped down my cheek, but I refused to give him the satisfaction of seeing that I was in pain. I kept my face as expressionless as possible, even as my cheek stung.

He bent down closer, his face mere inches away from mine.

His lips parted and he was about to speak when instinct took over. Stiffening my fingers, I thrust them toward his right eye.

I was shocked that I met my mark. I'd expected his reflexes to be too quick for me to do any damage. Perhaps he just thought me so weak that I wouldn't even attempt to fight back.

He groaned in pain and clutched his right eye, giving me the two seconds I needed to push past him and scramble toward the door. The door was closed, but the lock had been damaged thanks to that Joseph man who had stormed out of here earlier. I started dashing along the corridor, skidding and slipping on the shiny floors as I ran with speed that took my breath away. I headed straight for the exit of Michael's apartment. My heart pounded as I slammed up against it. I gripped the handle and try to open it, but it was locked.

Oh, God.

I looked around frantically for a key, but found none. I couldn't spend any more time looking. I kept expecting Michael to race up to me and grab hold of me at any second. I gripped the handle again and pulled down as hard as I could. To my shock, the handle snapped off and I was able to push the door wide open. I might not have had the strength of a vampire, but whatever I had become, I was stronger than I could have imagined. It was an uncanny feeling to possess such strength while having done nothing to earn it. It was like… magic. My whole body had transformed into this bizarre species that I hadn't even known existed until only hours ago.

I could hear Michael cursing in the background as I dashed off down the wide veranda. I must have hurt him quite severely.

I'd had to defend myself once like this before, in my neighborhood back home. I'd gone out to the convenience store too late one evening, and on my way back, someone had tried to mug me. I'd jabbed him in the eye. God knew what would've happened that night had my reflexes not been so fast.

I had no idea where I was running to. I just kept speeding as fast as I could.

I threw a look over my shoulder, fearing that

Michael would already be chasing me. Thankfully he wasn't—yet. I ran round and round the circular veranda, and when I reached the elevators, I entered one and traveled upward to the very highest level—the one directly beneath the trapdoor that Michael had brought me down through. I hurried up the winding staircase and began fumbling with the latches. The metal clanked and was so noisy, it was a struggle to work in silence. Every time a voice came from down below, my heart jumped into my throat.

Please, open up.

I have to escape.

I still had no idea where my sister was, but if I went looking for her, I would end up getting caught and then there would be no hope for either of us, or Hassan. I had to call for outside help, somehow get the attention of those tanks that were set up not far away. I believed now more than ever that they had to know about this coven of vampires. Otherwise why would they be so near?

This door proved much harder to budge than Michael's door had been. But to my relief, just as an elevator creaked, I managed to open it.

As soon as my feet dug into the sand of the desert, the brand in my right arm began to burn. I had to pause for a moment to get a handle on the pain before hurrying forward again through the dark. I bit my lip, trying to focus on the boundary in the distance, where it appeared the sun was out. After I had traveled perhaps five miles, to my horror, I hit an invisible barrier. I didn't know what I'd been thinking. Perhaps, as a half-blood, I would be able to walk right through, just as the vampires seemed to be able to do. But that wasn't the case. I ran all around the area hoping that there would be at least one weak spot, but it was hopeless. I tried screaming and shouting for help. Nobody answered. The tattoo on my arm continued to burn mercilessly. I looked back toward the entrance of The Oasis and was relieved to see that nobody had followed me out yet. Perhaps the groaning of the elevator had been someone descending to the lower levels, not coming up to me.

The thought of willingly returning down there made me shiver. I was surprised that Michael hadn't already followed me out here, but I suspected that he would be looking for me around the atrium, perhaps with a dozen other vampires, just waiting to punish me.

Still, I had no other choice. There was no way I was going to break free through this barrier.

I hurried back across the sand, hoping that at least nobody had noticed me come out here. I reached the entrance, but before climbing back down the iron staircase, I looked around to see if anyone was on the platform beneath me. There was nobody. Gathering all the courage I could muster, I began my descent down the staircase, easing the trapdoor shut above me. Once I touched back down on the floor, I crept to the nearest wall of glass and looked around at the atrium. I could see several vampires milling about along the verandas, but nobody seemed to be in any particular hurry.

With their sense of hearing, I would've been shocked if nobody had detected me leaving, not to mention hearing my screaming above ground. Perhaps nobody had paid it any mind because for whatever reason, half-bloods couldn't pass through the invisible barrier the same way vampires could.

I took a deep breath as I walked back into the elevator. It was clear there was no escaping to bring help from outside. I had no choice but to figure out how to help myself from the inside.

I had this time away from Michael—time I couldn't help but think would be horribly short-lived—and I had to do what I could to locate my sister and Hassan. I prayed that Michael hadn't been lying to me when he'd said that my sister was okay.

I descended all the levels of the atrium until I reached the ground level. I had no idea where to even start, but I figured that the ground floor was the logical place. I ran into a rose garden and crouched down among the bushes, barely even breathing as I listened as hard as I could. I was hoping that I'd overhear some snippet of conversation that could give me an idea as to where she could possibly be.

There were a number of conversations going on in the chambers surrounding me. But one in particular caught my attention, perhaps because it seemed to be the closest one to me, only ten feet away. Keeping low against the ground, I crawled through the bushes.

Ouch.

I looked down at my forearm to see a line of blood. I instinctively raised it to my lips and sucked on it, hoping that my saliva would help it clot faster. I almost choked. My blood tasted... horribly bitter. Then I noticed something that made me doubt my eyesight. My wound was beginning to heal before my very eyes. Soon I would never even have guessed that I'd scratched myself in the first place, had it not been for the bloodstains on my skin. I reached up to touch my cheek where Michael had cut me earlier with his claw. The skin felt completely smooth—again, as if there had been no cut in the first place.

This isn't real.

What other powers does my new body possess?

I tuned in again to the voices surrounding me, particularly the conversation going on ten feet away. It was hard to make out what they were saying, because there were multiple conversations going on at once and the voices blurred into each other.

I moved closer, looking all around me to be sure that there were no vampires, before leaving the rose garden and heading straight for the veranda. I kept close to the wall until I reached the door where the conversation was coming from.

From the sound of it, they were eating and talking at the same time. A delicious smell wafted from the room. Even though my stomach was in knots, it still grumbled. I hadn't eaten properly since the day of the dig, before Hassan and Lalia had been kidnapped.

I listened for about a minute longer, but when I was unable to pick up on anything interesting, I motioned to move away and continue listening in another part of the atrium. But then the door clicked open and an elderly woman appeared behind it. Her white hair was tied up in a tight bun.

I feared at first that she was a vampire—I still wasn't sure how to tell the difference when a vampire's fangs and claws weren't extended. But as a smile spread across her face, she looked like the friendliest person I'd come across so far in this ghastly place.

"You look lost," she said. "Are you one of the new recruits?"

I wasn't sure whether to stay and respond to her, or

run. But something about her evoked trust in me, so I nodded. "Yes."

She stepped back from the door and opened it wider so I could see into the room. There was a crowd of people—if I could call them people—sitting around a long rectangular table. They had plates of food in front of them and were eating away while chatting.

"Are you hungry? Would you like to join us?" the woman asked. "I'm Pamela, by the way. I'm a half-blood too, in case you couldn't tell."

Although my stomach could have done with some food, I still didn't think I had enough of an appetite. But I nodded all the same and let her lead me inside. I was still thinking about Michael lurking around looking for me. Going into this room with these half-bloods might hide me from him a little longer and I could ask them about my sister.

"When did you get here?" Pamela asked.

I wasn't sure how much time had passed. A part of me had been avoiding thinking about it, because it only made me feel more desperate about Lalia.

"Just very recently," I replied, my voice stiff.

"Where were you taken from?" another half-blood asked—a girl who looked no older than thirteen.

"Just from the desert outside," I replied.

"Whose half-blood are you? Or perhaps you're just a general servant like most of us here?"

"A vampire named Michael took me in."

No sooner had I said the words than a hushed silence fell around the table and all eyes fixed on me.

I stared back at them. "What?"

"Michael Gallow," a man in his forties replied. "And he made you his slave?"

"Apparently." I was beginning to feel impatient. "Please, I need your help, if there is anything you could tell me at all—my sister, she's been taken—"

The middle-aged man stood up from his seat, his hands clenched into fists. He looked from me to the rest of the half-bloods sitting around the table.

"What's the matter?" I asked, uneasy.

The atmosphere was suddenly electric with tension.

"We don't know that Michael is definitely going to get rid of one of us." Pamela set her fork down on the table. "Calm down, Frederick."

"Don't tell me to calm down." The man glared at the old woman, then looked round the table. "What are you waiting for? This is Michael's new muse, for whom one of us slaves is going to be sacrificed by the end of the week."

My stomach flipped.

Oh, no.

I didn't need a lot of wit about me to know that it was time I left this room. I darted for the exit, but four male half-bloods formed a wall in front of it, blocking my way. Each of them held knives. Then they began to approach me.

"I don't know if this is a good idea," Pamela said, eyeing the men. "You might all get into more trouble than it's worth if you touch a half-blood Michael has already claimed as his own."

The rest of the half-bloods in the room acted as though they hadn't even heard Pamela speak.

"Pamela's right," I said, trying to keep my voice steady. "I wouldn't do this if I were you." I didn't want to show fear, because fear was the first sign of defeat. I'd just survived several encounters with blood-sucking vampires, I couldn't allow myself to be finished off by a group of half-bloods.

Five of them lurched toward me at once. They were fast, just like me, but I managed to throw myself under the table in time to miss their blades aimed directly at my chest. More half-bloods chased after me, trying to grab me as I emerged at the other end of the table. The room was small, and there was only one of me. I knew my tactics were just a way to delay the inevitable— unless I managed to reach the door in time.

I might have been safer with Michael after all...

I tried to make my way toward the exit, but I was hopelessly outnumbered. I'd managed to fight my way within five feet of the door when a man lurched for my midriff and sent me crashing to the ground. Straddling my waist, he raised a bread knife and brought it down toward my heart. If I hadn't forced my leg upward and kneed him in the groin, the blade would've sunk right through me.

He backed away from me, doubled over in pain, and I scrambled to my feet again. Fighting my way to the door, I pushed it open and staggered out. I headed straight for the rose garden and dove into a cluster of bushes, ignoring the thorns scraping my skin. I tried to keep hidden within the bushes as I scrambled away, but a strong hand closed around my ankle, dragging me out of the bushes toward the clearing in the center of the rose garden. Another large man stood over me, and while he wasn't armed with a knife, his fists were like iron balls as they began pounding down against my face. They were merciless, and by the sixth blow, I felt close to unconsciousness. Any second now, another person would arrive and hand him a knife. This would be my end...

"What are you doing?" A deep voice spoke.

The man on top of me didn't let up his pounding. If anything, he hit me with more vigor. My eyes were so puffy and bloodshot, I could hardly see through them.

"Why are you beating this girl?" The voice spoke again, more aggressive this time.

I barely heard the half-blood's answer. All I was aware of was the pain coursing through me, and the pounding of blood in my ears.

Then I felt arms beneath my body. I was lifted from

the ground by a man and he began carrying me away from the gardens. He sped up and then the sound of an elevator filled my ears. We ascended several levels, and after walking some distance along another veranda, a door clicked open.

I began to struggle. Whoever this man was, I couldn't believe that his intentions were anything but evil. Just like everyone else in this godforsaken place.

I groaned as he laid me down on a bed, my battered limbs brushing against the mattress.

His weight pressed the bed downward by my side, and then the man's face appeared above mine, staring down at me.

"Don't hurt me," I gasped. "Please."

A cold hand touched my forehead, and then withdrew. My ears caught the sound of slicing flesh. I feared for a moment that it was my flesh, and I was just so numb that I couldn't feel it. But when the man's wrist pressed against my mouth and cool blood trickled into my mouth, I realized that he'd just cut himself. I coughed and spluttered. His blood tasted even more disgusting than mine.

"You're a wreck," he said. "Stop spitting out my blood. Drink it. It will speed up your healing."

I still didn't know whether to trust him, but the thought of relief from the pain was enough to make me begin swallowing his blood. I held my nose to make the taste more bearable, though the strange texture of it remained off-putting as ever.

Within a minute of drinking the man's blood, a miracle happened. The pain all over my body and face subsided. My vision returned to me. I found myself staring up into the face of a handsome dark-haired man with vibrant green eyes. It was the same man who'd stormed out of the sauna earlier, after Jeramiah had asked him to half-turn me.

"Joseph?" I said, sitting up slowly and backing away toward the headboard.

He nodded, then stood up from the bed.

I stared at him, studying his face and trying to figure out whether he was any danger to me now. I wondered what his agenda was in saving me from those half-bloods. His face was quite expressionless as he looked me over. It was hard to come to any kind of conclusion.

"So you're… a vampire?" I asked.

He nodded.

"Why did you help me?"

"Because I saw them beating you into a pulp for apparently no reason."

I narrowed my eyes on him. "Why would that bother you?"

He paused, frowning as if he were unsure of the answer himself. Then he shrugged. "It's what any man would have done who wasn't a total monster."

So you're not a total monster?

"What are you going to do with me now?" I asked.

"I'm not going to *do* anything with you. In fact, it's best you leave. Are you coupled with a vampire?"

The thought of leaving made me panic. I still didn't trust this vampire, but so far he hadn't given me any reason to fear him.

"A vampire called Michael stole me and brought me down here." I bit my lower lip. "Please… don't make me leave. He's going to put me through torture when he finds me again."

A flicker of discomfort played across Joseph's face. "So Michael hasn't been treating you well?" he asked.

I gathered my knees to my chest. "He's a sick bastard." That was all I wanted to say of Michael. I was trying to forget the trauma he'd put me through. I didn't want to relive it over again.

"Where did Michael steal you from?"

"The desert. They also stole my sister and a friend. I was out looking for them. I walked right up to that weird barrier, and Michael pulled me through it... Who are you exactly?"

He paused before responding. "Joseph Brunson."

It irritated me that his name was all the information he offered. "And? You seem to be different than the other vampires I've met here so far. Why did you storm out of the sauna the moment you saw me? I thought you were going to attack me."

He averted his gaze away from me. "Long story," he said darkly.

Although I was curious, now certainly wasn't the time for long stories. This vampire, for whatever reason, was behaving sympathetically toward me and didn't seem to be as crazy as all the others I'd met here so far. I had to take advantage of the situation while I could.

"You must know where the humans are kept in this place, right?" I asked. "Do you have any idea where my sister might be?"

He took a seat on the edge of the bed, still keeping his distance from me, and breathed out slowly. "Humans are kept in the basement beneath the atrium. But simply knowing this isn't going to be of much use to you."

My heart lifted a little, even as my anxiety increased. "The basement? Can you take me there?"

He furrowed his brows. "What's your name?"

"River. River Giovanni."

"River," he said, a deep frown still on his handsome face. "Even if I knew exactly which cell she was being kept in, and you managed to get her out of the prison without alerting anyone, and then up through the many levels of the atrium which is swarming with vampires who can detect human blood miles off, you still couldn't escape. The boundary surrounding The

Oasis won't let you out."

"C-couldn't you help us through the boundary? You're the only sane person I've come across so far in this place. Could you not find it in yourself to help us?"

He breathed out impatiently. He shot a glance toward the door, as if to check nobody was standing there, and then spoke in a low voice. "If I knew a way out, I wouldn't be here myself."

His answer took me by surprise. "What do you mean?"

"I can't pass through the boundary either."

I stared at him, wondering if he was just lying to me. "But you're a vampire?"

"Yes. And not all vampires have permission to come and go as they please."

I was trying to wrap my mind around his words. "So you're... you're a prisoner here too?" I asked disbelievingly.

"You could put it like that."

"How long have you lived this way?"

"I've lost track of time down here, but it hasn't been

long."

I leaned a little closer toward him. "Have you tried to escape?"

"How else would I have discovered I couldn't pass through the boundary?"

His words dealt my hope a crushing blow. If he, a vampire, couldn't figure a way out of here, what chance did I have?

"So there's really no way out of here?"

"There is no immediate way out."

"What do you mean?"

"An escape will require time and planning," he replied so quietly he was practically mouthing. "And even then, of course, there's no guarantee."

"And have you been planning to escape? Surely you can't be happy living here forever. What have you discovered so far? Is there anything I can do to help—"

I jumped at a banging on the front door. My eyes widened in panic.

Joseph froze, staring at the door, then looked back at me.

I scrambled off the bed and rushed over to him,

gripping his shoulder. I dared not speak but mouthed instead. "Please, if that's Michael, hide me. Keep me here. I beg you, don't let him take me."

He looked reluctantly from me to the door again. It was impossible to know what was going through that mind of his.

There was another round of banging and then Michael called, "Open up, Joseph."

Somehow he'd managed to find me. Perhaps one of the half-bloods had told him that Joseph had taken me away.

I was relieved when Joseph grabbed my arm, pulled me out of the bedroom, and led me along the corridor toward the farthest room, which happened to be… a sauna. I knew by now that vampires didn't need saunas, so I wondered whether Joseph had a half-blood of his own already.

Silently, he pushed me inside and closed the door. I pressed my ear against the wood, listening to his footsteps disappear down the corridor.

The front door opened.

"You have my half-blood," Michael said.

"*Your* half-blood?"

"Yes, *my* half-blood," Michael replied irritably.

"The same one you left to be beaten by a gang of men?"

"Just hand her over, Joseph," Michael snarled. "She brought it on herself by running away from me."

"And what made her run away?"

"That's none of your business… You seem to forget, vampire, that I am one of the rulers of The Oasis. I suggest you hand over the girl now lest you sorely regret it."

"Please," Joseph said. "We both know who really runs this place."

I heard a scuffle, the banging of a door, something smashing against a wall. Then Michael swore loudly, and Joseph spoke again. "Come on, Michael. We've never been the best of friends, but surely we can settle this like gentlemen. Why don't we go to Jeramiah and see what he has to say."

I froze.

Jeramiah?

The same vampire who let Michael have me to begin

with?

What is Joseph thinking?

"Agreed," Michael said, his voice strained.

"Wait here," Joseph said. "I'll get her."

No. No. No.

Footsteps approached, and Joseph opened the door to the sauna.

His shirt was ripped and rumpled, as though he'd just been in a fight, though there were no signs of cuts or blood anywhere.

He held out a hand for me to take.

"No, Joseph. You don't understand. Jeramiah is going to choose Michael."

"River," he said, looking at me sternly, "if you want my help, then you'll come with me."

I didn't know what else to do. I had no choice but to trust him. I reached for his hand, and took it. At least his strength gave me some comfort as his fingers closed around mine and he led me outside. I was glad that he continued holding on to me, even as we exited the corridor and appeared by the doorway.

I stepped behind Joseph, trying to hide myself from

Michael, as I eyed him warily.

To my surprise, his eye appeared to have healed already, though he looked like he had just borne the brunt of the scuffle between the two men. His arm had a deep gash in it, and his neck also looked red.

He glared at me, and I was only able to hold his gaze for a short while before I looked down at the ground and clutched Joseph's hand even tighter. I was grateful that Joseph kept me on the opposite side of him, away from Michael, as we left the apartment.

We traveled along the veranda in silence until we reached Jeramiah's front door. Michael knocked.

Footsteps sounded and the door creaked open.

The vampire with harsh blue eyes and dark shoulder-length hair appeared behind it, his eyebrows raised in surprise as he looked at the three of us.

"We are here to settle a dispute," Michael said. I winced at the confidence in his voice.

I looked up at Joseph's face. He seemed to be quite unfazed as he looked calmly at Jeramiah. I couldn't fathom what gave him such confidence. I just prayed that it was founded on something other than male ego.

"Joseph has claimed my half-blood as his," Michael said.

Jeramiah's eyes fixed on me, and then he looked back at Joseph.

"What is this, Joseph? I thought you said you weren't interested in a companion?"

"I did say that. But I've changed my mind."

"How come?"

Joseph ran a hand through his thick dark hair. He breathed out a sigh that I was sure was exaggerated. "I regret not being able to do what you requested of me earlier. My confidence evaporated as I was locked in the room with a human… this girl. Her blood called to me and I didn't think that even you would be able to restrain me. I was sure that I would end up killing her. I know now that I have a very serious problem, but I want—and need—to solve it if I'm to be of any real use to The Oasis… I think the only way I can overcome my problem around humans is with a half-blood assisting me. The bitterness of her blood will help me."

As Jeramiah stared at Joseph, I wondered for a moment whether he doubted Joseph's story. "But why this one? There are others you could have."

Joseph glanced down at me. "Because… I've taken a liking to this one. She's newly half-turned, so she and I have much in common. We're both getting used to these supernatural bodies and I think we might make a good team."

Jeramiah frowned. I was sure that he was about to refuse Joseph's request, but then his eyes softened and he shrugged.

"Michael," he said. "Just let Joseph have her. He's been having a rough time adjusting and this might help him to finally be of some real use to us."

Michael looked furious, but surprisingly, he didn't argue with Jeramiah. *It seems that Jeramiah really does wear the pants in this place…*

Michael glared daggers at both Joseph and I and, without another word, turned on his heel and stormed away.

"I do have a condition though," Jeramiah said as Michael disappeared.

I held my breath.

"What's that?" Joseph asked.

"We still have one human left to half-turn from the most recent batch. Prove your theory. Take this girl with you and half-turn a healthy human. Let's see if you can control yourself."

Joseph's tension seemed to spread from his jaw down to his hand, which squeezed mine tighter.

There was a pause. I had no idea what he was going to say.

The thought of my assisting in half-turning someone was the most horrific thing I could imagine. And yet, if Joseph refused, I'd be stuck with Michael. I tried to justify that the human would be half-turned anyway— just by another vampire, who I guessed would be much more insane than Joseph.

Joseph seemed to have come to the same conclusion as he said, "Certainly." I was amazed by the confidence in his voice.

"Good," Jeramiah said, a contented expression on his face. "Let's do this right now."

Chapter 12: Ben

What have I gotten myself into?

I hadn't been able to see any way out of the situation.

I'd realized on the way to Jeramiah's apartment that River being a half-blood could be used as an advantage both for herself and for me in escaping. After I'd refused to half-turn anyone in front of Jeramiah, I saw no way of suggesting that I join them on a hunt in the near future. Because what reason would Jeramiah have to trust me after my behavior?

Then, after realizing how off-putting River's blood had become to me after her half-turning, I'd seen just how we might be able to help each other.

But it had backfired.

I had of course expected Jeramiah to put my theory to the test. But I'd thought he might wait until the hunt itself, once we were already outside of the boundary, not have me experiment on a human beforehand.

Although I felt guilty about inflicting on another human the life of a half-blood here in The Oasis, with no guarantee of who might take him or her on, Jeramiah had made clear that the person had already been chosen to be a half-blood. Either I did the job, or someone else would.

Now I just had to hope that my theory would indeed hold up, because there was no way out of this now.

Jeramiah, River and I made our way down to the ground level and Jeramiah led us into a room where a woman was huddled in one corner.

I've got to pull through this.

I can't murder again.

Having hot human blood within such close proximity immediately stirred the predator within me, even as I tried to put it back to sleep. I wanted nothing more than to sink my fangs into her and never let go. I clutched River's arm and held her closer to me, breathing in her scent deeply, hoping that her bitterness would blur out the sweetness of the human less than five feet away.

Once I felt a little more confident in moving closer, I did, still holding River close to me, until I was standing right next to the cowering woman.

I knew what to do—I had already half-turned Tobias, after all. I knew how to inject my venom, and at what moment to pull away. But that was just the problem—summoning the willpower to pull away. Taking one last deep breath of River, and then holding my nose so that her scent would remain with me longer, I bent down quickly. Grabbing the woman, I dug in my fangs.

She squirmed and cried beneath me, but I held her tight. As blood began to seep into my mouth—fresh, hot, exhilarating blood—any small confidence I'd felt evaporated. There was no way I could stop myself from taking another gulp of blood, and then another and another. I was going to finish this woman off, and not even Jeramiah would have the strength to pull me off.

"That's enough blood, Joseph," Jeramiah commanded as he gripped my shoulder. "Release your venom now."

I heard him, and yet I couldn't find it in myself to obey. It seemed like a sin to poison this blood, so pure and divine. To turn something so sweet into something so bitter and rotten.

The woman began to grow weak beneath me, her struggling lessening. A few more gulps, and she likely wouldn't have the strength to survive the half-turning—I would've made her too weak to make it to the other side even if I could find it in myself to release my venom.

Then a wrist slid between my nose and the human's flesh. A cold, smooth wrist. As I breathed in, it smelt disgusting. River's scent was mixing with the blood that I was drinking, making it less palatable.

I drew back, swallowing the gulp that was already in my mouth, but not feeling such an appetite to go back for more.

My mind returned to me, along with my willpower to not let this be a failure. I clutched River's arm and breathed heavily against her skin again before once again plunging my teeth into the woman's neck. I refused to suck this time, and instead inserted my ice-cold venom into her bloodstream. I drew away before it felt like I had begun—as Jeramiah had once instructed me—and, holding River by the waist, I buried my head in her neck. I breathed her in for the final time before darting out the door.

If I had performed it correctly, the half-turning would now be in process and the human would be shaking. But I didn't want to stay any longer than I had to. I headed for the gardens and stopped once I was in the center of the willow orchard.

I leaned against the trunk of a tree. Exhaling and inhaling, I tried to calm myself after the frenzy that I had just managed to break free from… thanks to my new half-blood friend.

I looked up to see River approaching. Her expression was a mixture of fascination and horror as she stared at me. I must have looked a state, with blood dripping from my mouth and staining my shirt.

"Did you do it?" she asked in a hoarse whisper.

I nodded slowly, finding my voice.

"I think we did."

Chapter 13: Ben

River waited with me a while longer as I recovered my senses beneath the willow tree. After ten minutes, the door to the room where I had half-turned the woman opened, and Jeramiah stepped out. He made his way directly toward us.

I was relieved to see that he had a satisfied expression on his face.

"It looks like you did the job," he said, looking from me to River. "The human is showing all the right symptoms. Seems you two do make a good team."

"Good to hear," I replied dryly.

"I'll check back on the human tomorrow morning. As for you, feel free to take the girl back to your place." He winked at me. "She's yours now."

With that, he headed off.

River and I stood in silence, just looking at each other.

"Thank you," she whispered.

I didn't need her thanks. When I had caught sight of her being beaten by a man almost twice her size in the gardens, I hadn't thought twice about going to her aid.

She was pretty, with large turquoise eyes and long dark hair. Physically, I'd been attracted to her as soon as I saw her in that sauna. Her looks had only made it harder to control myself around her. That was one of the reasons I'd darted so quickly from the room.

But I'd realized only afterward that saving her in that rose garden had been a way of helping myself. I'd been so shrouded in darkness recently. I'd murdered so many people—more than I'd even been able to keep count of—and my bloodlust was still as strong as ever. Taking this girl under my wing was helping me keep my head above water. Her blood not being tempting in the slightest, she reminded me of what it was like to not feel like the devil personified around someone who happened to be weaker than me.

And now, if I dared to believe that we might be close to being invited out on a hunt, my escape wouldn't be possible without her.

I cleared my throat. "You're welcome," I replied. "Shall we return to my place then?"

She nodded and took my hand again.

As we entered the elevator, I asked, "So where are you from originally?"

"New York," she replied. "You?"

"California," was the easiest answer I could give.

"Vampires… To become one, you get turned? Who turned you?"

Admitting that it had been my father would only invite another slew of unwanted questions. Besides, I still didn't know this girl well enough to trust her—certainly not enough to reveal my true identity. So I gave her a similar answer to the one I'd given Jeramiah when he had first asked me.

"I came across a vampire one night—I was attending a friend's beach party. Apparently he thought of me as an easy target. He drugged me and when I woke up... I was this."

She gasped. "My God. Why do vampires do that? Turn people? What's the point?"

I shrugged. "Guess they want to increase their kind."

"How did you get here? To this place?"

"I met Jeramiah and some of his companions in Chile."

I could see that she was still in a state of shock. None of this had fully sunk in yet.

"Did you have any idea about the existence of supernaturals before coming here?" I asked.

"I mean... I had seen footage on the TV, but I never believed any of it. I just thought it was some kind of elaborate hoax. Do other supernatural creatures really exist too? Witches? Dragons?"

"I don't know about dragons," I answered, surprised. "But witches, werewolves and ogres certainly do."

She looked dumbstruck.

Reaching my door, I pushed it open and we walked

inside. I looked down at her as we stood in the entry hall. "Are you hungry?"

She bit her lower lip. "I probably should eat something. I was invited to join that group of half-bloods for a meal, actually… But in case you couldn't guess, I didn't get far into it."

I smiled. "I don't really have anything, uh, suitable for you. Unless you like the idea of drinking blood?"

"Blood?"

"Yes. I drink human blood." I thought it best to just tell her upfront.

Her mouth dropped open. "That's all you drink?"

I knew that my answer would only disturb her about her sister, but she would find out sooner or later. "That's why vampires kidnap so many humans. A few of those they capture are turned into half-bloods, and the rest they keep down in the basement… I'm pretty sure they're all for blood."

"Oh, no."

"How old is your sister?" I asked.

"Six."

She needed to eat something or she would get sick. I

had to think of something to comfort her with or she'd have no appetite for anything.

"If your sister is only six, I think she might be safe for a while. They have gone to the trouble of kidnapping her, they might even wait until she's grown to maturity before thinking about taking her blood…"

Of course, they could also have kidnapped her for her tender young blood. But River didn't need to hear that now. I'd scared her enough already.

"Michael said that she wouldn't be harmed," she said, her voice cracking.

"Then maybe my guess is correct…" I needed to change the subject. "You're actually in luck. Unlike vampires, half-bloods can consume regular food. You don't have to drink blood."

"Thank God."

"I don't have any regular food in my own fridge, but…" I thought about where the best place would be to get some food for her. Then I remembered my neighbor who'd been friendly to me recently—Lloyd. He'd said that I could come to him if I needed something.

"Come with me. Just a few doors down, Lloyd, my neighbor, has a half-blood staying with him. He should have regular food."

She nodded, though she still looked petrified.

We headed for the door, and just before I opened it, she took my hand again. The idea that she got comfort from me brought me warmth. That I was still capable of experiencing emotions like this was in itself comforting to me.

I stopped with her outside Lloyd's apartment.

We didn't have to wait long after knocking. He opened the door and the moment he saw me, he smiled.

"Hello, Joseph. You've been keeping to yourself a lot recently, haven't you?"

"Yes. Until now, actually…" I gestured toward River. "She's my new half-blood friend. I realized that I have absolutely no food for her in my kitchen. Do you have some to spare?"

"Yes, plenty. Come in."

We stepped inside and he led us to his kitchen—which looked pretty much identical to mine. He gestured toward the fridge and looked toward River. "What's your name?" he asked.

"River," she replied, even as she kept close to me.

"Beautiful name…" He looked back at me. "Would you mind seeing yourself out after you are done? I was actually in the middle of something."

"Yes, of course. Thank you," I said.

I took a seat at the kitchen table and watched as River opened the fridge and scanned the shelves.

Food. It felt like an eternity since I had last tasted it. While a part of me yearned for it, the other part was repulsed by the idea of putting anything but human blood in my mouth.

Judging by the ingredients River was picking out, it looked like she wanted to make herself some sandwiches. She gathered a loaf of whole wheat bread, cucumber, lettuce, cheese, and some kind of pickle. After she was done, she closed the fridge door.

"Finished?"

"Yes."

We left Lloyd's place and headed back to mine. I took a seat again at my kitchen table and watched as she went about preparing sandwiches.

She worked in silence, and then sat down at the table opposite me and began eating.

I watched her expression as she swallowed.

"This is weird," she said, as she stopped chewing. "Food. It tastes… different." She dunked a spoon into the jar of pickles and dolloped more into her sandwiches. "Everything tastes more… tasteless. It feels like it needs more salt or more… something…"

"I guess that's because you're halfway to being a vampire."

"Do you know a lot about half-bloods?" she asked.

"More than you, I'm sure, but not a lot."

She adjusted her shirt to reveal a tattoo—the same black cross that we all bore—etched into her right arm.

"What is this?" she asked.

"I don't know. Everyone who enters The Oasis seems to get one the first night they're here."

"I tried to ask Michael about it, but he was cryptic."

Marilyn had also given me no clear answer. I'd put it down to just her being drunk. But I hadn't bothered to ask anyone else about it. I had been so focused on how to escape this place.

After River had finished eating, and chugging down a whole jug of water, we went into the living room. Sitting down in the comfortable armchairs, we continued talking. She began asking dozens of questions about vampires, half-bloods and the world of supernaturals. I tried to answer them to the best of my ability without giving away too much personal information. I also deliberately skirted around the topic of immortality because I felt it would overwhelm her.

The excuse I'd given to Jeramiah for wanting River—that she was newly turned and so we had much in common—had been something that I'd thought of on the spot. But it turned out to be true. Although I'd been surrounded by supernaturals all my life, from the very day of my birth, being a supernatural myself was still so new to me.

When she asked me whether she could ever turn back into a human again, assuming we managed to escape, I didn't know how to answer her. Of course, I knew that there was a cure for vampires, but half-bloods? That was uncharted territory. I hadn't even known of the existence of half-bloods until I'd met Jeramiah. Discovering a cure to vampirism hadn't been easy, and had come about after dangerous experimentation. I just answered her honestly.

Then she began to shiver.

"You're cold?" I asked.

She nodded.

"Feel free to use the sauna," I said.

She stood up. "No, I'll just get myself a blanket."

She walked out of the room and returned with a thick duvet. I guessed she had found it in one of the spare rooms.

She took her seat again in the armchair and wrapped herself in it. She shuddered. "This cold. I've never experienced anything like it."

There was a knock on the door.

River looked panicked. I wondered who it could possibly be. Leaving her in the living room, I made my way to the door and opened it.

There was no one there. I looked left and right, but the veranda was empty.

But then my eyes lowered to the floor in front of

me. A backpack had been placed in front of my doorway. I bent down and picked it up, then made my way back to the living room.

River was standing waiting for me, the duvet still draped around her shoulders. Her eyes widened as she spotted the backpack in my hands.

"That's mine," she whispered, taking it from me. "Who brought it here?"

"There was nobody outside," I replied.

"I left this in Michael's apartment. I wonder why on earth he'd bother to bring it back to me after everything…"

She sat down and unzipped the bag, pulling out a vial of clear amber liquid and then a black fabric bag. Loosening the bag, she revealed that it was full of gold coins.

"In Michael's place," she said, looking tense, "when I woke up after being drugged, this bag of coins and this vial of liquid were waiting for me in his bedroom. There was a note left with them. It said that these were gifts for my mother and my brother. Michael said they were gifts from The Oasis. Why on earth was I given these? How do they even know about my family?"

I stared at the two objects. I was just as clueless as her.

"I'm sorry," I said. "I have no idea."

She put the backpack down and looked at me. "When do you think the next hunt will be?"

"There was one recently. It could be a week or maybe longer until they go on one again. There doesn't seem to be a set schedule."

She moved closer to me, the blanket trailing behind her on the floor.

"Please, help me locate my sister. Even if we have no way of saving her yet... I just need to see her."

I looked down into her desperate eyes and heaved a sigh.

"Okay. I'll help you."

Chapter 14: Ben

After promising River I would try to get us down to the basement, I now had to figure out how.

I didn't need to examine the lock again to know that I wouldn't be able to break through it without damaging it. It was far too complicated a lock to pick.

No. We had to find a smarter way to do this.

River took a shower while I thought, and by the time she'd finished, I'd come up with a plan.

She stepped into the room, dressed in new clothes—a crisp white blouse and cotton pants.

"Any ideas?" she asked anxiously.

"Yes. We're going to need to pay another visit to Jeramiah."

She looked confused, but didn't ask questions. Perhaps by now she trusted me enough.

We left the apartment and headed to Jeramiah's place. When I knocked on the door, an ebony-skinned half-blood girl opened it.

"You're here for Jeramiah?"

"Yes."

She looked over her shoulder and called back into the apartment. "Baby, it's Joseph and his new half-blood."

Jeramiah approached the door. He had a smirk on his face. "We're seeing a lot of each other today."

"I won't take up much of your time," I said. "I've come to request a visit to the basement."

"Why?"

"I know River can help me cope with one human. I want to see how I cope surrounded by crowds of them. If I do end up accompanying you on a hunt, I'll need to be prepared for this."

I was surprised by how easily he agreed. "Yes, that's not a problem. But I will send someone to accompany you. You're permitted half an hour only."

Half an hour. I hoped that would be enough time. It would have to be.

Jeramiah called back into the apartment. "Lucretia."

Lucretia—his new girlfriend, apparently—walked back to the door.

"What?"

"I want you to accompany Joseph and his girl down to the prison. I've given them permission to walk around there for thirty minutes. You don't need to accompany them down. You can wait in the room upstairs if you prefer—just make sure they have returned after half an hour."

"Okay," she said, eyeing us. "I'll be with you in a minute. I'd like to get something to do while I'm sitting there."

Jeramiah disappeared back into the apartment, while River and I waited for Lucretia. She only kept us waiting a minute. She arrived holding a cosmetic bag and slipped out the door.

We descended the levels of the atrium and arrived in a familiar room, where the entrance to the basement was. She pulled out a key from her pocket and opened the lock, then pushed the door open. The smell of human blood was overwhelming. I reached for River's hand and breathed in her scent. Together we descended the steps, leaving Lucretia at the top, where she sat down in one corner and began to file her nails.

Arriving in the first prison chamber, we began walking from cell to cell. The cells' doors had windows, but they were fixed quite high up and River was too short to see through them. So I scanned all the windows first, and if I saw either a young man who fit the description of her friend, Hassan, or a girl who could have been her sister, I lifted River up to the window so that she could peek through.

We traveled from chamber to chamber, careful not to miss a single cell. When I had last been down here, I had been in more of a hurry, and although I'd run fast, I'd barely scratched the surface of the number of prisoners down here. After scanning six entire chambers with River, I was beginning to wonder whether half an hour would indeed be enough time. Especially because I felt the need to keep stopping and breathing in River's scent in order to keep myself sane.

Finally, at the end of a row in the seventh chamber we passed by, River breathed, "That's him. Hassan." She was pointing to a young man curled up in a cot.

She banged on the window pane. Apparently he was fast asleep.

She banged more loudly. "Hassan! Wake up!"

The man stirred finally. His expression was that of utter shock as he gazed up at us through the window. He shot to his feet and hurried toward the door.

"River?" he gasped, his Middle Eastern accent thick. He pressed his hands against the glass. "Can you get me out of here? Please!"

River looked up at me. "Is there no way we could take him upstairs? We could hide him in your apartment."

I shook my head. "I wouldn't risk it. We still don't know how we're going to escape, and his life could be in more danger than if he just stayed here."

Hassan's body was trembling. "This place is a

nightmare," he said.

"We're going to come back for you," River said. "I promise."

"When?" he asked desperately.

River looked up at me, then back at the young man. "I don't know. But... as soon as possible." She leaned closer against the glass. "Do you know where my sister is?"

He shook his head sadly. "I have no idea. I'm so sorry."

River swallowed hard. "Okay. We're going to have to keep looking for her. Just... try to keep yourself well. I promise I'll come back as soon as I'm able to."

He looked devastated as we left him and continued walking along the corridor.

"Lalia?" she whispered. "Where could she be?" Then she began to shout out her sister's name. "Lalia! Lalia! Where are you?" Her voice echoed around the prison.

I gripped her shoulder. "Don't shout," I said, my voice low.

We sped up, moving faster past each of the cells. We didn't have much time left. We were on our thirteenth chamber of humans and we still hadn't found her.

"My God. Where is she?" River looked like she was about to have a nervous breakdown.

I gripped her hand hard. She needed to keep a cool head or there was no chance of her being reunited with her sister.

And then I spotted a little girl with long brown hair, two doors along. She was lying on a cot along with another girl who looked in her late teens.

I gestured toward the door and, holding River by the waist, lifted her up so she could see through the window.

"Lalia!" she gasped. She slammed her fists against the window.

The little girl stirred on the mattress, then looked toward the window. Her round young face looked dumbstruck, as though she was in a dream. Then she leapt up and rushed toward us. She was far too short to reach River's level. But her small hands banged against the door and she cried out her sister's name. "River! Help! I want to go home!"

The older girl in the cell with her woke up and

moved toward Lalia. She wrapped her arms around Lalia's midriff and picked her up so that she could be level with her sister.

River looked at me desperately. "Is there really no way we can take her with us now?"

"No. Lucretia is waiting for us upstairs. There's no way we could smuggle anyone out unnoticed."

River looked desolate, but she didn't argue with me.

It was uncomfortable watching the two converse through the glass. River kept comforting Lalia telling her that we'd find a way to get her out.

I didn't know what River was thinking in making such a promise to her.

River and I might be able to figure out a way to escape this place, but smuggling Hassan and Lalia out with us posed another set of obstacles entirely.

CHAPTER 15: RIVER

No words could describe how painful it was seeing my sister on the other side of the glass. I didn't know who that other girl was, but I was grateful that at least Lalia hadn't been imprisoned alone. Lalia didn't appear to be sick or wounded, but her face betrayed trauma that I feared had scarred her for life.

When Joseph touched my shoulder and said that our time was up, it killed me to step back.

Leaving Lalia in that cell was the hardest thing I'd ever done in my life.

As Joseph and I exited the chamber her cell was in, my legs felt weak. And as we reached the bottom of the staircase that would lead up to the exit of the prison, I broke down. I sank to the floor, pulling my legs up to my chest and burying my head against my knees.

I was thankful that Joseph gave me space even though we were late leaving the prison. He just waited for me until I composed myself. When I looked up, he reached down a hand to me and helped me up. I wiped my eyes, doing my best to avoid looking like I'd just been crying, and we continued up the stairs.

Lucretia was waiting for us, still working on her nails in one corner of the room. She looked up as we entered. Then she got to her feet and dusted herself off.

"You're almost ten minutes late," she said, looking at us pointedly.

"Apologies," Joseph replied. "We got lost. It's a really huge place down there. How many cells are there altogether?"

She shrugged. "No idea… So how did it go?"

"It went well," Joseph said. "River's blood is a real help to me."

"Good," she muttered, locking the entrance to the prison again and sliding the key into her pocket.

We left the room and stepped out into the brightly lit atrium.

We parted ways with Lucretia and headed back toward Joseph's apartment. I was unable to speak a word. My mind kept replaying those few moments I'd spent with my sister, how forlorn she'd looked, and how utterly helpless I'd felt to do anything to help her.

As we entered Joseph's apartment, he broke the silence.

"It's late. I suggest you get some sleep."

I almost scoffed. Sleep. That was the last thing on my mind. Even though my body was exhausted, I doubted I would even be able to get a wink of sleep tonight.

Still, since Joseph was turning in, I did too. He showed me to one of the spare bedrooms in his apartment, then left me alone and returned to his own room.

I looked around the spacious bedroom and flopped down on the bed. It was one of the most comfortable beds I'd ever lain on. Here in The Oasis, everything exuded luxury. The floors, the bed linen, the lighting... and yet I couldn't enjoy any of it.

I was beginning to feel uncomfortably cold again, my bones starting to ache. I slid beneath the blanket and curled up into a fetal position, closing my eyes tight and praying for my sister.

I tossed and turned, trying to find some relief in sleep, but I might as well have prayed for a miracle.

I was still trying to fall asleep well into the early hours of the morning.

It must've been about 2am when a strange noise broke through my thoughts. I sat up in bed, holding my breath as I strained to listen.

It sounded like a machine giving off an odd grinding noise. And it was coming from one of the levels below. I wondered what on earth it was. I got out of bed and padded over to the door. Opening it, I walked down the corridor and approached the front door, then placed my ear against the wood.

Yes. It sounded like someone was grinding something. And it was loud, at least to my sensitive ears.

Since I wasn't able to sleep anyway, I was curious to go and see what it was, but I didn't dare leave the apartment by myself. I didn't want to wake Joseph either, so I didn't see any other choice but to head back to my bedroom.

I jumped as Joseph's bedroom door creaked open. His dark hair was tousled, and his nightshirt hung loosely, revealing his muscular torso.

"You couldn't sleep either?" I whispered.

He shook his head. "I rarely sleep in this place… Do you hear that?" he asked.

"Yes. That's why I'm out of bed," I replied. "Do you have any idea what it is?"

"I'm going to check it out."

"I'll come with you," I said. Anything was better than going back to bed and lying there in silence with nothing to distract myself with.

Joseph opened the front door softly and we began following the noise. It led us down several levels until we realized that it was coming from the ground floor. We descended quietly and soon realized that the sound was emanating from one of the chambers directly opposite the lily pond.

I exchanged glances with Joseph. He held a finger to his lips.

My mouth sealed, I controlled my breathing to make as little noise as possible as the two of us made our way over to the door. Joseph bent down as soon as we reached it and peered through the narrow keyhole. I waited patiently until he had finished looking and gave me a turn.

The room was dimly lit and running the full length of the furthermost wall was a huge piece of machinery. Hovering next to it was a tall man. I couldn't see his face because his back was turned toward me, but I recognized who it was based on his hair and physique. Jeramiah. His hands were obscured by a wide metal funnel, but it looked like he was lowering something into the machine, and each time his hands descended, that loud grinding noise penetrated my eardrums.

What is he doing?

I remained watching for about a minute longer, and then I looked back at Joseph. He gestured with his head toward our right, suggesting that we leave, and I followed him. We walked quietly, and didn't speak again until we were back in his apartment. Even then, we spoke in hushed tones.

"That was weird," I said.

"Yeah," Joseph said grimly. "A lot of things about this place are weird."

"What do you think he's doing?"

"I don't know."

It was frustrating. There seemed to be far more things about this place that Joseph did not know than those he did.

I was reminded of another question that I'd been meaning to ask him. "This tattoo, it started burning when I tried to escape through the boundary. Why was that?"

He leaned against the doorway, running a hand over his own right arm.

"The same happened to me," he replied. "I thought for a while that the witches here might be responsible for these tattoos. But after staying here a while longer, I'm really not sure..." He held my gaze for a few moments and then looked away. "I'm going back to bed. Good night."

He headed toward his room.

Watching him disappearing down the corridor filled me with emptiness. Though he was still a stranger to me, his presence brought me comfort. And I wasn't used to sleeping alone. I was seventeen, and although it was embarrassing to admit, I was so used to sharing a room with my two sisters, I actually didn't like sleeping alone.

"Joseph," I said, just before he closed his door.

"What is it?"

"I was wondering, would you mind if I just... slept on the floor in your room? I'm just not used to sleeping alone, to be honest. Especially not in a strange place. I don't think I'll ever get any sleep..."

He looked taken aback by my request. He looked back into his room, and then pushed his door open wider. He shrugged.

"All right. If you want."

"Thank you."

I hurried back to my bedroom and grabbed my

pillow and blanket. I was going to carry these to his room first and then come back to drag the mattress. But when I stepped into Joseph's bedroom, he had already stripped his bed of its pillows and was setting up a sleeping area on the floor for himself.

"Oh, no. Joseph, I don't want to kick you out of your bed. I don't mind sleeping on the floor."

He turned around and gave me a smile. Dimples formed on his handsome face.

"It's all right, River. You sleep on the bed."

I felt guilty as he continued to set up his sleeping spot on the floor, but I wasn't going to object to him acting like a gentleman.

God knew, I hadn't known enough of them in my life.

Chapter 16: River

After I moved into Joseph's room, I was amazed that I managed to get a few hours of sleep. And I woke up feeling refreshed. Perhaps that was just one of the many quirks of this new body I found myself inhabiting, that I didn't need much sleep. I guessed that vampires didn't need much either. Joseph was up before me. I found him in the kitchen, sipping from a glass of blood.

He eyed me as I entered. "How are you feeling?"

No matter how well rested I was, it was impossible

to feel anything but miserable knowing my sister was still trapped in the basement of this horrifying place.

"A bit better than last night," I muttered.

I moved to the fridge, and opened it. There were still some sandwich ingredients left over. I placed some bread, cheese and tomatoes on a plate, poured myself a glass of water, and sat down opposite Joseph. Even as I began eating, I couldn't take my eyes off the blood he was downing.

It was disconcerting to think that that blood could easily have been my sister's or Hassan's.

"I don't understand how you can drink human blood," I said, shuddering.

Joseph wiped his lower lip with a napkin. "It's not a question of choice. At least not for me."

"What do you mean?"

"Some vampires can survive on animal blood alone, although it tastes disgusting compared to human blood. But I can't stomach anything but human blood."

"You have some real self-control issues."

"Glad you finally noticed," he muttered.

"But how do you live with yourself? I mean, you used to be human. How can you just drink that every day and not be crushed by guilt?"

His jaw twitched. "What makes you think that I don't feel guilt?"

I didn't reply. I guessed he was just doing what he had to do to survive. If I'd been in his position, I probably would have done the same.

I shifted in my seat, wanting to lead the conversation elsewhere. I could see I'd made him uncomfortable.

"Before when you were answering my questions about vampires, you mentioned that you can't go in the sun. What would happen if you did?"

"We would wither away eventually," he replied. "We can stand it for only so long."

"What about half-bloods? Can they tolerate the sun?"

"I don't know how well, but I'm sure better than vampires."

I was about to ask another question when someone disturbed us by knocking on the front door.

Joseph got up and left the kitchen while I continued

eating my breakfast.

As the door opened, Jeramiah spoke. "I've just come from checking on the half-blood you created. She's doing well. You released just the right amount of venom."

"Good," Joseph replied.

"A couple of things. First, there will be another party upstairs tonight. I know you said you weren't interested, but now that you have a, uh, companion, perhaps you'll reconsider? Anyway, think about it. Secondly," he continued, "our next hunt probably won't be for a couple of weeks. But I've been thinking that since you've been putting effort into learning to control yourself around humans, we could go on a small hunt, just a few of us. We can always do with a few extra humans and it would be good practice for you. What do you think?"

"I like the idea," Joseph said, without a moment's hesitation.

"No witches would come with us, since it's last minute and they usually only agree to come on the main hunts… This means we're at risk from the hunters as soon as we step outside the boundary, but there will only be a few of us and if we move fast, we should be all right."

"I'm willing to take the risk," Joseph replied. "When were you thinking to go?"

"Tonight after the party."

Joseph paused this time for a few seconds, then said, "Sure."

"Good," Jeramiah replied. "If I don't see you aboveground tonight, I'll stop by your door later on to pick you up—along with your half-blood, of course. The party should wind down around 2am. So let's say 3am."

"We'll be ready."

Then the door closed.

I'd forgotten all about my food by now. I'd even forgotten to swallow what was already in my mouth.

My jaw hung open as Joseph returned to the room. He looked at me.

He didn't bother recounting the conversation. He knew that I heard everything.

We had less than twenty-four hours.

I shot to my feet and looked at him desperately. "We have to find a way to get my sister and Hassan out of the boundary."

A frown formed on his face. Then he sat down in a chair opposite me and rubbed his temple, deep in thought.

How are we going to do this? How can we bring them on a hunt with us? Joseph and I might be able to figure out how to escape once we were outside the boundary, but how would I save my sister and Hassan?

Yes, we'd know the exact location of the place to give to the police, but how would they break in? There was an impenetrable boundary protecting The Oasis. If we didn't find a way to get them out, my sister would be stuck here forever. Or until they decided to murder her for her blood.

I slumped back into a chair, burying my head in my hands as I tried to think of how we could possibly get out of this situation.

A wave of relief rushed through me when Joseph looked up ten minutes later and said:

"I think I have an idea."

Chapter 17: Ben

It was possibly the most harebrained scheme I had ever thought of, but I didn't see what other option we had.

After I explained it to River, her face filled with doubt, but she apparently didn't have any better ideas, so she agreed.

We had some hours until the party tonight, so in the meantime we discussed how we were going to pull off the idea. We talked in hushed voices, practically mouthing, about all the things that could go wrong, and how we could avoid disaster.

Once River and I could hear sounds of people gathering upstairs for the evening's revelry, I took her into the kitchen. Grabbing the container of pickles from the fridge, I emptied the remaining pickles into a bin, then washed and dried the container.

I sat River down opposite me at the table and placed the container in the center between us. Then she held out her wrist for me. Extending my claw, I slit through her skin, deep enough so that blood began to flow into the container. Once I was sure that I had enough, I wrapped her wound up in tissue, then made her drink my blood. Her body did have its own natural healing capabilities, but they weren't as fast as those of a vampire, and it was best that she healed before we headed upstairs.

After her wound closed up, River went to change. She managed to find a long red gown in one of the bedrooms, while I just wore a loose shirt and cotton pants.

Then we left the apartment and headed upstairs. I slid an arm around her waist as we approached the crowd. There were tables to our left, lined with half-bloods serving up blood and liquor, and there was also a self-serve snack area containing regular food to our right.

A trio of witches were in one corner with instruments, playing a haunting melody for those in the central dance area.

I led River into the midst of the dancing couples and placed one hand on her waist while taking her other hand in mine. I swayed her slowly from side to side even as I scoped out our surroundings. I was looking for Jeramiah, and so was River.

I spotted him first.

He was one of the dozens of vampires sitting on the soft cushioned seats. He was talking to a group of three vampires while Lucretia sat on his lap.

I was glad that Jeramiah and his girl were surrounded by people. It would make it easier for River to do her job.

I turned River around so that she was facing Jeramiah.

"You see him?" I breathed into her ear.

She nodded. I felt her gulp against my chest.

"Let's go," she whispered.

Still holding hands, the two of us casually made our way toward where Jeramiah and Lucretia were sitting with their companions. He raised his glass of blood to me as he spotted us.

"You came."

I forced a smile and sat down in one of the cushioned chairs near to him. River took a seat next to me, and her eyes fixed instantly on Lucretia. Once Lucretia met her gaze, River gave her a smile and to my relief, Lucretia smiled back.

That was the first step.

I busied myself with a glass of blood that one of the half-blood slaves handed me as I continued to watch River. She left the seat next to me and moved closer to Lucretia.

As Jeramiah continued his conversation with the male vampires sitting next to him, I realized that I was sitting only a few feet in front of Lloyd. I'd been so fixed on Jeramiah, I hadn't even noticed him until now.

Lloyd nudged my shoulder and engaged me in small

talk. I responded, grateful that I now looked like I was busy, while my attention was focused on the conversation that River had started up with Lucretia.

River was beginning to ask questions about life as a half-blood—questions she had already asked me. Lucretia responded kindly. Another good sign.

After about twenty minutes of chatting, River suggested that they get something to eat from the snack table. Lucretia agreed. She kissed Jeramiah, then took River's arm, and they both made their way over to the food.

Even now, Lloyd was continuing to talk to me. Fortunately, he seemed to prefer the sound of his own voice to mine. I just nodded and grunted occasionally.

Lucretia was serving up different snacks to River, advising her on what she might like, and then the two of them stood to one side and ate as they watched couples dancing. After they finished their snack, they chatted some more and finally River shivered, rubbing her shoulders.

"I'm freezing," she said. "Aren't you?"

Lucretia shrugged. "Not particularly… But I

wouldn't mind some time in the sauna. I've been out here for quite a while already and the desert air can be cold at this time of night."

"Should we go to Joseph's sauna, or Jeramiah's?" River asked.

"Jeramiah's is closer," Lucretia replied, taking the bait.

The two of them left the area and disappeared from my sight as they headed back down into the atrium.

I waited three minutes, then left Lloyd with the excuse that I needed some time to prepare myself mentally for the hunt later on.

I left the area as fast as I could without appearing to be in a hurry. Descending the stairs toward the atrium, I took the elevator down to the level where Jeramiah's apartment was. I hurried forward along the veranda and stopped at the sight of the two girls standing outside Jeramiah's quarters. Lucretia had pulled out a key, and was just in the process of opening the door. Lucretia pushed it open and the girls stepped inside. The door was seconds from closing when River said, "I'll shut the door."

I raced to it within seconds. River was keeping the door ajar, waiting for me. As soon as she felt me holding it, her hand disappeared and she continued down the corridor with Lucretia toward the sauna.

I waited until their voices had faded, and for the sound of the sauna door opening and closing.

Although they were in the sauna, I still had to be silent. Half-bloods' hearing might not be as sharp as a vampire's, but it was still acute.

Easing the door open only enough for me to squeeze through, I slipped inside and left the door resting on its latch.

Then I looked around the dark apartment.

Keys.

Where would Jeramiah keep his keys?

Chapter 18: Ben

I'd been careful to look Jeramiah over when we were upstairs, looking for any bulges in his pockets, but I hadn't seen any. I hoped that meant his keys were in his apartment.

Moving silently from room to room, I began looking in every cupboard, in every drawer, and on every shelf that I came by. I stopped every now and then, tuning in to the conversation that River and Lucretia were having in the sauna to make sure that they were still occupied. It wasn't until I reached the room at the very back of the apartment, some kind of storage room, that I found a large cluster of keys hanging from a hook in the wall.

Removing them silently, I placed them into my pocket. Then I continued searching the rest of the apartment for keys, and on finding no more, I had to hope that the ones in my pocket would be all that I needed.

I crept back through the apartment and slipped back out through the door. Again, I was careful not to close it fully, resting it against the latch so that it remained ajar.

Then I headed straight down to the ground floor. I ran across the gardens to the room that held the entrance to the prison. Before entering it, I looked inside to make sure that it was empty. Then I crossed the room and lowered to my knees so that my eyes were level with the lock.

I splayed out the keys in my palms, looking at each of them and trying to decide which to try first. I opted for a large bronze one. It didn't fit. Then a thinner black one. Still no luck. I tried four more keys before finally arriving at the right one. I breathed a sigh of relief as the lock clicked open. I hurried though the door and locked it behind me from the inside.

The smell of human blood was intoxicating on this side of the door. Fumbling for the container of River's blood in my pocket, I pulled it out and opened the lid. I inhaled its bitter scent, trying to calm my nerves. Then, stirring the liquid around, I put the container to my lips and tipped some blood onto my tongue. I closed the lid again and returned the container to my pocket.

Holding my nose and keeping the disgusting blood on my tongue, I hurried forward into the depths of the prison. I headed first for Hassan's cell, since it was on the way to Lalia's. Looking through the window, I saw that he was huddled in a corner, knees drawn up to his chest, his head buried in his hands.

I spread out the keys in my palms again and looked at them. These cells would have to share a common key. There were just too many in this prison.

It took me ten keys before Hassan's cell door clicked open. Hassan gazed up at me, stupefied. Then he rushed toward me. I shot away from him, backing up against the opposite wall.

Breathing deeply, I hissed, "Keep your distance from me!" I took another sip from River's blood, then looked back at him. "I'm here to help you. But I'm also a risk to you. Wait here in your cell while I fetch River's sister. I'll knock on the door when it's time to come out. Understand?"

He looked bewildered, but nodded.

Then I darted off. Although River's blood in my mouth was helping to overwhelm the scent of human blood surrounding me, just the sight of a human so close to me was enough to ignite my bloodlust. I dreaded arriving outside Lalia's cell. *Her young flesh would be so tender to sink my fangs into, her blood so pure and sweet…*

My hands shaking slightly, I opened the container of River's blood again and took another swig. I'd consumed half of it already. I had to pace myself. If we got held up for some reason and I ran out of River's blood… That was a scenario I didn't want to think about.

I tried using the same key that I had used for Hassan's cell for Lalia's, and it worked. The door swung open, and Lalia and the older girl who was with her looked toward me in shock. Then relief washed over their faces and they rushed toward me just as Hassan had done. I leapt back down the prison corridor.

"Where's my sister?" the little girl asked.

"I'll take you to her," I whispered, my voice strained as I tried not to tempt myself by looking at her. "Just follow me, okay? You can come too," I added, addressing the older girl.

Careful to keep at least ten feet between us, I led the two girls through the winding network of cells, urging them to hurry up every now and then. It was frustrating that I couldn't just pick them up and carry them both myself. The other girl ended up carrying Lalia on her back, which made things a little faster.

Arriving at Hassan's cell again, I was glad to see that he was waiting inside his room and opened it only when I knocked. He looked at me, and then at the two girls. I backed away again, now with full access to three humans.

I lengthened the distance between them and me even more, and continued traveling back toward the exit. We reached the stairs and I opened the door again before we hurried into the small room. Still maintaining as much distance from them as possible, I instructed them to huddle in one corner as I fumbled with the keys and locked the door once more. River's taste was beginning to fade from my mouth again. I took another swig from the container. Now I barely had one full mouthful left.

I cursed myself. I should have thought to take more blood from her.

We had to move fast.

As we stepped outside, I had to hope that we wouldn't bump into anyone on our way back to my apartment—and that nobody would notice three humans were missing from their cells before the hunt tonight. There were so many humans down in that prison, my hope didn't seem too unreasonable.

There was no way that I was going to get into the same elevator with them, so I called two elevators to the ground floor simultaneously. I stepped into one of them while they bundled into the other. I instructed them which floor number to press, and then we ascended. We arrived on the right floor at the same time. The doors slid open. I rushed out before they could and, running up ahead of them, ordered them to follow me. Hassan picked up Lalia and carried her on his back as they raced after me, trying to keep up with my speed. Rushing to the door of my apartment, I opened it and then ran down the hallway. I waited in the doorway of my bedroom for them to arrive.

"Shut the door behind you," I whispered as they entered.

Hassan did so. Then all three eyes fixed on me. Their faces were deathly pale and sweaty with fear.

"Now listen to me," I said, looking at them sternly. "Take a left down the corridor, and at the very end you will see a sauna. Lock yourselves in there and don't make a sound. Do you understand me?"

They all looked petrified, but nodded.

"Where's my sister?" Lalia whispered, her eyes wide with fright.

"I'm going to get her."

I waited until they hurried down the corridor and stepped into the sauna. When the door clicked shut, I approached it and, reaching into my pocket for the last of River's blood, I poured it into my palm and then spread it up and down the wooden door, hoping it would help to mask the scent of hot human blood at least somewhat if a vampire passed by.

Then I washed my hands in the kitchen and ran back out the front door. I headed straight back to Jeramiah's apartment. I was glad to see that the door was still ajar, as I'd left it. Pushing it open, I slid inside.

To my discomfort, River and Lucretia had left the sauna by now. I heard their voices coming from the living room. Creeping past, I was careful to hold the keys in such a way that they didn't clink and made my way back to the storage room at the back of the apartment. I replaced the keys on the hook in the wall slowly, rearranging them against the wall to look how I remembered finding them.

Now I have to get out of here.

I was about to head back to the front door to leave

when I heard a sound that chilled me to the bone.

The front door slamming.

And then Jeramiah's voice emanating from the hallway.

Chapter 19: Ben

"Lucretia?" Jeramiah called through the apartment. "Why was the front door open?"

Footsteps sounded as Lucretia made her way along the corridor toward Jeramiah.

"It was open?" She sounded confused. "Oh, I'm sorry. River said she'd shut it."

"River?"

"Yes. Joseph's half-blood is here with me."

More footsteps.

"Hi," River said. I could detect the nervousness in

her voice.

"Why are you two down here? Come up and enjoy the evening with everyone else."

"We were cold," Lucretia said. "We just had a session in the sauna and then we got to chatting in the living room."

"Well you can continue talking upstairs," Jeramiah said. "I'm just down to check on the new half-blood again, and then I'll join you."

No.

My eyes fixed on the keys dangling from the hook, then I looked around the storage room for somewhere to hide. It was small and although cabinets lined the walls, they weren't large enough for me to hide inside.

"Okay, I'll see you back up there," Lucretia said, and footsteps moved toward the front door. Then more footsteps proceeded toward me.

I backed up into the furthermost corner of the room. If Jeramiah stepped inside, there was no way he wouldn't spot me. He was a split second from entering as the door creaked. Then Lucretia's voice sounded again.

"Jeramiah?"

The door stopped moving.

"What?" Jeramiah called.

"River's just cut herself on the doorstep. Could you lend a bit of your blood?"

"All right."

I thought for a moment that he was going to fall for the distraction and leave, but to my horror the door continued moving until it was wide open.

I was bracing myself to be seen when his arm shot into the room. He reached for the hook and grabbed the keys, then disappeared again, his footsteps fading down the corridor.

Once I sensed him move to another part of the apartment, I crept to the door and looked out. The corridor was empty, and I could hear voices coming from the living room. I could not have felt more grateful to River than I did at that moment. She must've moved herself in there on purpose, to grant me a clear exit through the front door. Without another moment's hesitation, I hurried out of the storage room, silently racing toward the hallway. The door was ajar again—perhaps also River's doing after she'd cut herself. I looked down at the step on my way out. The sharp marble ridge was lined with her bitter blood.

I launched into a sprint and didn't let up until I arrived back outside my apartment. Breathing heavily, I leaned against the doorway and looked back across the atrium toward Jeramiah's quarters. I wasn't ready to enter my apartment yet—not with those three humans locked up in there. I had run out of River's blood to distract myself.

I remained watching Jeramiah's front door. After five minutes, he appeared, keys clasped in his right hand, and he made his way toward the elevators that would take him down to the ground floor. River and Lucretia exited the apartment soon after him. There was no sign of a limp from River—Jeramiah's blood must have finished healing her.

If River followed the plan, she'd stay upstairs for another twenty minutes or so, and then come back down again. I had no choice but to wait in silence.

I caught sight of her across the veranda almost forty minutes later. Her face was tight with worry as she made her way toward me.

"Did you find them?"

I looked around, unwilling to speak a word out here. I just nodded and led her inside the apartment.

"They're in the sauna," I whispered.

Her face lit up and she motioned to rush there at once, but I gripped her hand and held her back. "I need some more of your blood."

I took her into the kitchen and placed the container in the center of the table. She winced as I cut her skin again with my claw and filled the container with more blood. Then I set the container aside and raised her wrist to my mouth. I closed my lips over her skin and sucked. I was careful not to swallow too much, so that some blood remained in my mouth, soaking my tongue. Then I healed her wound by feeding her more of my own blood. Even with her blood in my mouth, I still wanted to stay as far as possible from the humans. I didn't want to tempt fate.

"This is so weird," she said, eyeing the container of her blood with disgust.

"Better than watching me slaughter your sister," I muttered.

Chapter 20: River

I hurried to the blood-smeared door of the sauna and pushed it open. On seeing my sister safe there with Hassan and the other girl she'd shared a cell with, I burst into tears. Lalia jumped into my arms, clutching me tight as I showered her face with kisses.

"Oh, my God, River!" Lalia gasped. "Why are you so cold?"

I didn't want to start explaining to her. She'd been through enough trauma as it was. There would be time for that later.

"I've just been worried sick about you," I said, running my hands through her hair. "How are you? How's your asthma?"

"She had an attack," the older girl next to her said. "Some woman came in and helped her."

"What's your name?" I asked her.

"Morgan," she replied.

"Someone came in to help Lalia?" I asked. "Who?"

"She was a big fat woman," Lalia mumbled against my shoulder.

"And she helped your asthma? How?"

"She gave me some horrible juice."

"Juice?"

"Tasted real sour," she replied.

"And how is it that you two ended up sharing a cell together?" I asked.

"I guess because Lalia is only six," Morgan replied, "they didn't think it was wise to put her by herself."

Lalia was still holding onto me so tight she was practically choking my neck.

"So you're okay?" I said. "What have you been doing all this time?"

"Just sittin' on our butts," Lalia muttered.

I looked toward Hassan. "And how are you?"

He looked shaken. "As well as I can be, I guess—certainly much better than a few hours ago now that I've escaped that place."

"Where are we?" Lalia asked. "And who was that tall man who saved us?"

Again, I wasn't sure how to explain without freaking her out more than she already was. Once we were out of this place, I would explain everything to her.

I also realized that we'd been making too much noise. I raised a finger to my lips. "That tall man's name is Joseph," I whispered. "He's going to try to help us all out of here. But now, we just need to be quiet, okay?"

***

I spent the next two hours holding my sister in the sauna. I told her to stop asking questions, which she did. She seemed content to just be in my arms.

Then it was time for me to leave.

"I'll be back soon," I whispered.

"Huh? Where are you going?" Lalia looked panicked and clung tighter to me.

"I need to go speak to Joseph. I promise I won't leave you long. Just stay here and keep quiet."

Lalia looked like the last thing she wanted to do was let go of me, but I detached myself from her, and placed her in the furthest corner of the room on the bench.

I found Joseph pacing up and down in his bedroom, the container of my blood clutched in his hands.

He looked toward me as I entered.

"So... are you ready for what's next?" he asked, his voice deep.

I didn't know that I would ever feel ready for what we had planned next. But it was now or never.

"Yes," I said, with as much confidence as I could muster.

"It sounds like the party is dying down up there now," he said, looking up at the ceiling.

I followed him out of the bedroom toward the front door. He opened it and we both stepped out, looking around. Vampires and half-bloods were descending through The Oasis' entrance and heading back to their apartments. We remained standing by the doorway for the next fifteen minutes, until the last trickle of revelers seemed to have returned. But strangely, neither of us had spotted Jeramiah, Lucretia or Michael yet.

I looked back at the clock hanging from the hallway. It was already 2:30am.

We were running out of time.

I exchanged glances with Joseph.

"Where do you think they are?" I whispered.

He shrugged. "We just need to keep waiting."

Ten minutes later, all three of them finally descended. I wondered why they had taken longer than the others. I didn't give it too much thought though. I was just relieved that they had finally come.

I was expecting the couple to part ways with Michael once they arrived outside Jeramiah's apartment, but instead they remained standing and talking. Joseph and I looked away as Jeramiah turned, spotting us standing in the doorway.

Joseph's hands found my waist. He lowered his mouth to my ear. "Put your arms around my neck and pretend that you're kissing me," he breathed.

I stared at him, raising a brow.

Then I realized why he was asking this of me. Standing here doing nothing but staring looked odd. We needed to look like we were doing something.

Joseph positioned me in front of him, so that he still had full view of the trio. Slowly, I draped my arms around Joseph's neck and craned my neck upward. He leaned down until our lips were less than an inch apart. My breathing quickened as his green eyes met mine. He lowered his mouth to my cheek and pressed his lips gently against it, then averted his gaze back toward Jeramiah.

My skin tingled at the touch of his lips, so close to the side of my mouth. I hadn't expected him to touch me. But now that he was... I couldn't say that I objected. At all. When his hand rested on the small of my back, pulling me closer still, I felt butterflies in my stomach.

Geez, River. Get a grip.

He's just an... incredibly handsome guy.

"Are they still there?" I breathed, attempting to

distract myself from his touch.

He didn't respond for almost a minute as his lips continued to graze my cheek. Then he said, "They're gone now."

He loosened his hold on me and I took a step back. Our eyes locked before he cleared his throat and looked back through his doorway.

We both knew what had to be done now.

Chapter 21: Ben

I was thinking of River as I left her in the apartment and made my way up to the desert.

When I'd bent down so close to her face, her radiant eyes gazing into mine, I'd found myself drawing closer to her than I had either intended or needed to... without even realizing it.

I shook myself.

Stop being a fool, Novak.

Focus.

Arriving aboveground, I was glad to see that nobody

was still up here. Everyone had returned to their rooms. *Thank God.* It was 2:45am already. That left only fifteen minutes before Jeramiah knocked on our door. Fifteen minutes to get three humans up here undetected. We couldn't afford for anything to go wrong.

Sure that the area was empty, I ran back down to the atrium and headed back to my apartment. I found River alone in the living room, standing over a basin that she'd placed on a coffee table. She had already cut herself again and was draining more blood. I walked over to help her, slitting my own skin and allowing my blood to flow into the wide container. Both of our bloods mixed and formed a dark red pool at the bottom of it. Once I felt like we had enough, I healed her, then took a mouthful from the small container of River's blood in my pocket while she hurried toward the sauna to retrieve the humans.

I backed away, watching as she herded them into the living room. Walking to the basin, she dipped a hand in the blood and began to smear it over her sister. She looked toward Morgan and Hassan.

"Cover yourselves with this blood as much as you can."

The humans had looks of disgust on their faces—especially Lalia.

There wasn't enough blood to completely douse themselves with, but it was enough to dull their scent. It shouldn't be much more detectable than the other human blood that was stored in all of the vampires' apartments around The Oasis.

After the blood in the basin had been used up, I went into my bedroom and grabbed the dark beige rug that lined one corner of the floor. Rolling it up, I put it over one shoulder and then returned to the hallway to find that River had gathered the three humans to wait outside the door.

We had only ten minutes now before Jeramiah knocked.

I glanced at the three humans. I was going to have to carry two of them—the largest ones, Morgan and Hassan—while River would carry her sister.

This would be the closest I had ever been to a human without ripping out their throats since I'd

A WIND OF CHANGE

turned into a vampire.

I swallowed hard. River looked nervously at me.

Here goes…

I allowed Hassan to climb onto my back—it was lucky that he was shorter than me—and then I picked up the girl in my arms. Even with River's and my blood smothering them—as well as River's blood on my tongue—they still called to me like a siren, especially the girl.

Her neck was so close to my mouth. So painfully close. All it would take to have her warm blood flooding down my throat would be leaning down a few inches…

I forced the thought out of my head and was about to head out of the door when River said, "Wait!"

She put her sister back down on the ground, and hurried into the living room. Reappearing a few seconds later, she was clutching her backpack, which she flung onto her back. I supposed that taking the backpack was a good idea. River didn't know how long it would be before she reunited with her family. She might need money in the meantime.

River picked up Lalia again, so that the girl clung to her front like a monkey. And then we ran. I was so fast, I was sure that I was a blur to any onlooker. River was slower, but she wasn't too far behind me. Reaching the elevators, we hurried inside and made our way to the top. And then the final stretch of the journey... I carried Hassan and Morgan through the trapdoor and began speeding through the sand toward the edge of the boundary.

Six feet away from the exit, the brand in my arm began to burn again.

I looked over my shoulder to see River staggering, her face contorted in pain. Her brand was scorching her too.

What are these damn things?

It was almost as though they were conscious and were aware of our intent. I had been aboveground in the desert before without the tattoo causing me agony—like earlier this evening at the party. It only burned when it sensed that I was trying to escape. *It sensed.* I felt mad thinking of these tattoos as though they were conscious beings, and yet there was a clear pattern.

Clenching my jaw against the pain, I continued forward. As soon as we reached the boundary five miles away, I lowered Hassan and Morgan to the sand. Removing the beige rug from my shoulder, I waited until River had caught up with me and placed Lalia next to the other two humans.

"My God, River," Lalia gasped as she staggered around, apparently dizzy. "When d'you learn to run so fast?"

All she got from her sister in reply was a hush.

I dropped the rug and moved backward. The blood covering them felt like it was wearing off—or perhaps I was just becoming immune to it. I took another swig of blood out of River's container and breathed in deeply, desperately trying to distract myself from the humans' sweetness, especially the little girl's.

River picked up the rug that I had dropped. "Sit down in a huddle," she said. The trio did as requested and then she placed the rug over them so that they were somewhat camouflaged. Then River handed the backpack to Hassan for safekeeping.

We had just a few minutes to get back to the apartment now. I hoped that Jeramiah wouldn't arrive early. I scooped River up in my arms before sprinting back to the atrium. It was much faster than her trying to run after me.

Hurtling through the door of my apartment, I looked up at the clock. One minute until 3am.

River and I ran to the nearest bathroom and washed our hands. I looked at her clothes. They were stained with blood.

"You need to change," I said.

Her eyes roamed me. "So do you." She was right.

After we had washed our hands and faces, we found clean clothes. River ended up wearing one of my shirts, although it was far too large for her, and a pair of shorts—she hadn't been able to find any female clothes other than dresses.

Then, taking deep breaths, we waited in the hallway and stared at each other. I was sure that the same worries were going through our minds simultaneously.

Jeramiah had said that he planned to bring Michael and Lloyd with us. I had to capture one of them in order to get us through the boundary. I didn't know just how strong Jeramiah was, because there hadn't yet been occasion for him to display his full strength in front of me. But I knew that he was a Novak, and that was enough to know that I ought not underestimate him.

The plan was wild, and so many things could go wrong with it, but it was all we had.

Jeramiah ended up knocking two minutes late. I walked to the door slowly, and opened it.

His dark hair was tied up in a bun, and he was dressed all in black.

"Ready?" he asked.

He seemed sober. I guessed he hadn't drunk much at the party.

I looked over my shoulder and called to River. She arrived next to me.

Jeramiah smiled as he laid eyes on her.

"Good. Let's go."

That journey up to the desert was possibly the most nerve-racking experience I'd had since arriving at The Oasis. As we crossed the atrium, I looked down at the gardens below, my eyes traveling past Lucas Novak's memorial stone, and I wondered whether this would be the last that I saw of this place.

Aboveground, Michael and Lloyd were already waiting for us. I looked around, glad to see that no witch was present, as Jeramiah had mentioned. If a witch had come with us, our whole plan would likely have fallen to pieces.

My fists clenched.

We had hit the first obstacle. *How are we going to ensure we leave the boundary near where we left the humans?* There were any number of directions we could exit the boundary. We had to leave near them, or the distance we had to run could cause our plan to unravel.

I decided to just take the lead.

"Shall we start moving then?" I said briskly.

Holding River's hand and keeping her firmly away from Michael, who was glaring daggers at the two of us, I began to march toward the humans. Jeramiah looked a bit surprised at my initiative, but to my relief, nobody objected. They followed after me.

I sped up, and so did they.

"What time does the sun typically rise?"

"If we aim to be back by around 5am, we will be fine," Jeramiah said. "That gives us two hours—plenty of time to catch a few humans."

"Where do we plan to go exactly?" I asked, wanting to keep the conversation going as we approached the humans.

"The nearest town," Jeramiah replied. "It takes about fifteen minutes to travel there at our full speed. And we must run at our full speed if we want to travel past the hunters alive... So we'll have ninety minutes to look around the streets for any people out late."

"Hunters," River murmured. "Those men in tanks set up nearby... they're hunters?"

"Yes. They're the reason we typically travel with witches whenever we need to go out."

"Do you steal people from their homes?" River asked.

"Sometimes. It depends on how many humans we come across outside—"

Jeramiah stopped dead in his tracks. My breathing quickened as his eyes shot toward the three humans, now only twenty feet away.

That's it.

He's detected them.

I let go of River. "Go," I hissed to her. She darted toward the humans.

Lurching forward and grabbing Lloyd by the throat, I began hurtling after her. I ran with all the speed that my legs could muster, and I didn't look back once. When Lloyd tried to struggle with me, I dug my claws deeper into his flesh, then snapped his neck to paralyze him.

"I'm sorry, Lloyd," I muttered. I felt bad for doing this to him. He had only been friendly to me. But he'd been closer to me than Michael, otherwise I definitely would have grabbed the latter.

We approached within feet of the boundary, and I pushed us both full speed toward it. To my relief, we went flying right through it and tumbled down on the sand. Staggering to my feet and grabbing hold of Lloyd again so that I could pass through the boundary, I stepped back through where I sensed the humans were and grabbed Lalia by the hand. River had positioned all the humans in a row, linking hands with one another, while River stood at the end. I tugged on Lalia and stepped back out of the boundary again, pulling them all through with me... except River. I was expecting her to be holding on to Hassan's hand at the end of the chain, but he appeared without her.

She screamed.

I swore.

"Move back," I hissed to the humans, keeping myself in front of them, while still maintaining a grip on Lloyd.

Jeramiah and Michael stepped through the boundary ten feet away. Michael was holding River by the throat with one hand, while the other reached into her long hair and yanked her neck downward at a painful-looking angle.

"River!" Lalia screamed.

I positioned my claws over Lloyd's chest, above his heart.

"Let her go," I growled.

I looked from Michael to Jeramiah. While Michael's expression was nothing but vindictive, Jeramiah barely looked fazed at all. It was almost as if he had expected me to do this.

"Let the half-blood go," I repeated.

"Take him down, Jeramiah," Michael said, tightening his grip on River, who was beginning to groan.

I was expecting Jeramiah to lurch forward… or at least do something, but he did nothing. He just stood rooted to the spot, looking at me. Michael's claws were inching dangerously close to River's heart. I was about to shove Lloyd aside and dive for her myself when Jeramiah spoke.

"Let her go, Michael," he said, his voice steady.

Michael looked as shocked as I felt.

"What?" He gaped at his companion.

"I said let the girl go."

Jeramiah eyed Michael as he loosened his grip on her and stepped back, dumbstruck. Clutching her throat, River staggered across the sand toward her sister.

Then my cousin returned his gaze toward me.

"I thought you were grateful for us having taken you in," he said slowly. "Seems I was mistaken." He let his last words linger before continuing. "Well, I don't want to keep you here against your will, Joseph. So go on, take the half-blood and the humans... You're free to leave."

He spoke the last sentence louder, and the burning of my tattoo stopped. It was as if it had never hurt to begin with.

Jeramiah had an odd glint in his eye as he turned his back on me and headed back toward the boundary. Just before he reached it, he muttered beneath his breath: "Although something tells me you will be returning..."

I let go of Lloyd, whom Michael took hold of and dragged through the boundary behind Jeramiah, after shooting me a dirty look.

I wasn't sure what Jeramiah Novak meant by those last words. Perhaps he just thought that I wouldn't be able to survive the hunters outside and would come back begging to return, or perhaps one of the witches had put a binding spell on me, similar to the one my parents had once endured at the hands of Annora.

But something about the look in Jeramiah's eye as

he turned his back on me told me that it was neither of those things.

Something told me that after my weeks trapped in The Oasis, I hadn't even scratched the surface of what really went on here.

CHAPTER 22: RIVER

As I stood in the desert, rubbing my throat and watching the three vampires disappear through the boundary, I was overwhelmed by a mixture of confusion and relief. I had not the slightest clue why Jeramiah had let us go so easily, but I felt nothing but gratitude to finally be beyond the boundary of that terrifying place. And the fact that my brand had stopped burning only added to my euphoria.

I clutched my sister close to my chest, kissing the top of her head and holding her tight. Hassan returned my backpack, which I strapped on my back again. Joseph was still staring at the spot where the three vampires had left us.

Until now, we had been so focused on just how we were going to escape The Oasis, we hadn't talked about what we would do once we actually got out.

Now that we found ourselves free, so suddenly and so unexpectedly, I wasn't sure what our next step was.

For one, I wasn't the same person I had been on entering The Oasis. While I practically trembled with excitement at the thought of reuniting with my family again, I wondered what my life would be like now as this bizarre... creature. I guessed it was almost like being a human. I could still eat regular food, and be in the sun, at least for short periods. There were also perks I still hadn't quite wrapped my head around—like my superhuman speed and strength, and my heightened senses. I'd just have to find a way to cope with the aching cold...

I wasn't sure if my grandfather had told my mother yet that Lalia and I had gone missing—I assumed by now that he would have since days had passed. It made me ache inside to imagine how much pain she'd be in. She'd be worried sick. I couldn't wait to see the relief on her face.

But I was getting ahead of myself. We were still in the middle of the desert. One thing was for sure: I wanted to get as far away from this area as possible, in case Jeramiah changed his mind.

I approached Joseph and placed a hand on his arm. He looked down at me, his expression serious.

"What now?" I asked.

"Now…" He looked around the area, and his eyes fixed on a point in the far distance. "Now you need to reach the nearest town with your sister, Morgan and Hassan, and contact the police to take you back to your families. If you make your way to the hunters"—he pointed toward the area he was staring at, and I could make out the outline of tanks in a row—"they should help you get there. You are a half-blood, so they have no reason to harm you. You have no claws, no fangs, and are no threat to them or any humans whatsoever. Also, you have those gold coins, in case you need money."

My throat had tightened as he spoke. "What about you?" I asked.

"I must leave. It's not safe for a vampire to hang around here."

My mouth dried out.

There had been so much build-up to our escape, and then it had happened so quickly, the idea of parting ways and never seeing him again came as a shock. I hadn't had time to prepare myself for it.

Although we'd known each other for only a short time, it felt like I'd formed a stronger bond with him than I had with friends I'd known my entire life. He had been there during the most traumatic and darkest time of my life. For us to be torn apart so suddenly, so unceremoniously… it was hard to swallow.

"Wh-Where will you go?" I asked, my hand still resting on his arm as I looked up into his face.

"I'm not sure. I have some… things I need to figure out about myself."

I didn't want to let go of his arm. I didn't want our conversation to end. I didn't want to watch him race off into the darkness of the desert.

But I knew I couldn't keep him any longer. It was dangerous for him out here. He needed to leave.

So I just said, "Thank you."

He smiled, showing me his dimples for what would be the last time.

"You're welcome. And I should thank you too."

I moved closer to him and slipped my hands around his midriff. Resting my head against his chest, I hugged him tight. His arms wrapped around me and he hugged me back, his strength engulfing me. I felt teary as I looked back up at him. I reached for his neck and pulled his head down to my level so I could plant a kiss on his cheek. And then I stepped away.

"Goodbye, Joseph. It was… nice knowing you. If you ever happen to turn back into a human and like Lebanese food, you're welcome to visit me in New York any time. I, uh, don't really have a way to give you my number though…"

He chuckled. "That's okay. I'd have to track you down somehow… Goodbye, River."

Chapter 23: Ben

I didn't miss River's eyes moistening as I walked away. Truth be told, I was hurting to leave her too. But there was no point in dwelling on it. She had a different life to lead than mine. A very different life.

I still hadn't told her that she was immortal now, and a part of me felt guilty for it. It would come as a shock to her when it finally hit home. But now hadn't been the right time to tell her. She'd been too elated at finally escaping for me to drop such a bombshell on her. She would have to realize it on her own.

As I sped up along the sand, my ears picked up on a beeping in the distance, coming from the direction of the tanks. I had to get out of this area fast. The last thing I wanted was to escape The Oasis only to be recaptured by an army of hunters.

I was grateful that at least I didn't have the burning in my arm to distract me. I was almost too far away to make out the outline of tanks in the distance when a scream pierced the night air.

I skidded to a stop.

I knew that scream by now.

That was River's scream.

And then there was another sound that chilled me even more: Gunshots.

River. They're attacking her? But she's not a vampire. She's no threat to them.

Doubt upon doubt crowded my mind, but all of them were a waste of time.

I felt a crushing guilt. I'd been the one who had assured her that she would be safe with them.

"Bastards," I spat, as I began hurtling back toward the area.

As I got closer, I could make out a lone figure darting to and fro among the dunes with supernatural speed. River. Sprays of sand exploded all around her. She was dodging bullets.

"I'm coming, River," I breathed. "Hold on. I'm coming for you."

She began moving farther and farther away from the hunters, and I thought that she might be close to escaping their range entirely, when she let out another scream—strangled this time—and collapsed on the sand.

No.

No.

I pushed my legs harder, reaching the area just as tanks began closing in. I was a blur as I whisked past and scooped her off the ground. Another roar of gunshots exploded, spraying the sand all around me. One passed so close to my ear it practically grazed it. I raced away, holding River tight against my chest but not daring to look her over yet. I was scared at what I might see. Right now, I just needed to get her—us—as far away from danger as possible.

The minutes that followed were tense. I managed to escape the range of the hunters without being hit by one of their fatal bullets, but then I needed to find somewhere safe I could lay River down and examine her. The hunters' technology had clearly been developing rapidly and they had trackers that could detect vampires—it seemed that they could detect a vampire's presence for miles. I wouldn't have been surprised if helicopters started surrounding the area soon. And so I kept running until I came across a collection of small mountains that were indented with caves.

I chose the largest cave and carried River inside. I walked right to the back, and, after checking for snakes, placed her down on the ground. I removed her backpack so she could lie more comfortably. My eyes lowered to her right thigh. She was losing blood. Too much blood. A bullet had lodged inside her. I bent down closer to her. She groaned and squirmed as I eased the metal out of her and threw it aside.

It was a wonder that she was still alive at all. If this was one of the hunters' notorious bullets, it should have burned her up from the inside out. I could only assume that either this bullet hadn't been fired from one of their UV guns, or such bullets didn't have the same effect on half-bloods. It appeared to have just penetrated like any regular bullet.

Whatever the case, she wasn't looking good.

Lowering her shorts slightly, I checked that she was wearing underwear before removing the shorts completely. I needed to have full access to her thigh, and the shorts were getting in the way.

I took off my shirt and cleaned up her wound as best as I could with the cleanest corner of it. Then I cut my palm to feed her some more blood. Her face was still contorted in pain as she sucked my hand. Then she seemed to calm down a little. Although her wound was showing clear signs of healing, it took much longer than I'd expected. Only once it had fully closed did I allow her to attempt to sit up.

Putting my arm around her, I helped her upright. She looked in a daze. She stared at me with wide eyes, her lips parted, her breathing still uneven.

"Thank you," she whispered.

Chapter 24: River

When we approached the tanks, four men leapt out to see us. I explained to them that we had just escaped The Oasis, and they seemed to understand what I was talking about. They said they'd help us back to the police. But after they took Lalia, Hassan, and Morgan into one of the tanks, when it was my turn to get in, three hunters whipped out guns and aimed them toward me.

I didn't know what to think. I was just bewildered. Why were they trying to kill me? What had I done to deserve this? It was one of the most bizarre experiences of my life. To be treated like an animal, worse than a criminal—having committed no crime. Even after all the wrong my father had done, he had not been treated like this.

If it hadn't been for my new-found speed and lightning reflexes, I would have been shot the moment they pulled out their guns. I darted away from the tanks, away from my sister. I ran about the dunes, trying to dodge the bullets, until one caught me in my side.

When I fell to the sand, I was sure that that would be the end of me. The hunters would close in on me and lodge a final bullet in my head.

But then arms grabbed me, lifted me up from the ground and whisked me away.

Joseph. I still couldn't believe that he'd come back for me. I didn't understand why he bothered doing it, risking his life by coming right into the midst of the hunters just to save me—a girl he barely even knew.

After he brought me to a cave and healed me, although I was devastated at being ripped from my family once again, I was overwhelmed with gratitude for this young man.

"I'm so sorry," he said.

"It's not your fault," I replied.

"I should have given it more thought."

"There was no way you could have known."

"It seems they've adopted an absolutely zero tolerance policy for anything supernatural, harmless or not…" He paused, then asked, "How are you feeling?"

I looked down at my thigh. "Better."

"Did they take your sister and the others?" Joseph asked.

"Yes," I said, pain building in my chest at the reminder of my sister.

Poor Lalia. I didn't know that her nerves could take being separated from me once again. My only comfort was that at least this time, she wouldn't be surrounded by bloodsucking vampires and would hopefully be returned to our grandfather.

"There's nothing supernatural about them," I murmured, "so I just hope the hunters take them straight to the police."

I looked around the cave. There was a rattle coming from the far corner, near the jagged entrance. A rattlesnake, by the looks of it. I shivered, another wave of coldness intensifying in my bones.

"What now?" I asked, my voice unsteady.

"We need to leave this cave and reach the nearest town by daybreak."

I looked toward the sky outside. It didn't look like it would be long now before the sun rose.

"And then what?"

"Let's just get there first," he muttered. "With these hunters on patrol, we can't afford to get stuck in the desert. If we get caught out in the daytime, when I can't go in the sun without being blinded, they could have us trapped."

Joseph stood up, and, reaching down a hand for me to take, helped me up too. I replaced the backpack over my shoulders.

I was wearing nothing but Ben's shirt and my underwear, but my shorts were too torn to put back on, so I had no choice but to travel as I was.

"Climb onto my back," he said. "It'll be faster."

I was glad he suggested it. Although my thigh had healed, I was still feeling shaken and weak. I'd lost a lot of blood and my mouth was parched for water.

I climbed onto his back, feeling the taut muscles beneath his bare skin. Joseph's hands closed around my calves and secured me in place. Then, without warning, he shot out of the cave and began racing along the dunes again.

I kept my eyes peeled for any sign of the hunters. After ten minutes and God knew how many miles, the coast still seemed to be clear. Joseph had managed to shake them off, and I guessed that they were now searching for us in another part of the desert entirely.

Although I had so many things that I wanted to ask him, and seek reassurance about, I didn't speak to him as he ran. We both needed to concentrate.

He was the one who broke the silence. He stopped running and raised a finger.

"You see that?"

I strained to see where he was pointing.

Yes. I could see.

In the distance was the outline of buildings, the

outskirts of the city. And closer still was what looked like an early-morning market. There were poles sticking up, and wooden stalls being erected. I wasn't sure what day it was today, but the market seemed mainly for the locals. I couldn't imagine many tourists being up at this hour.

Joseph tensed.

I already knew what was going on with him. Human blood. I really wasn't in the mood for him to dig his fangs into me again, so instead I raised both wrists closer to his face.

"Do you think my scent is enough to block out the temptation?" I asked.

"If you keep close to me the whole time... I should be okay. I was while half-turning that woman..."

As we approached the market, I could make out the types of wares that were being sold. Mostly garments and shoes, with the occasional stall of dates and other dried fruit.

"We should stop here," Joseph said.

"Why?"

"For one thing, you're wearing no pants. We need to

draw as little attention to ourselves as possible, and that sure isn't going to help. I'm also half naked and in general look like I've just murdered someone. We'll use a gold coin to pay for clothes."

"Okay…"

Joseph cautiously approached the nearest clothes stall and set me down on the ground. He placed his arms around my waist, standing behind me with my back against his chest, keeping me close to him. I could feel his breath on the top of my head as he breathed me in while we moved closer to the stand.

The stall owner—a short woman wearing a hijab— gave me a disgusted look as I stood there half undressed. I ignored her expression. I was beyond caring at this stage.

I picked a black headscarf with a veil that covered my entire face except my eyes, and then a long black robe for the rest of my body. Then I looked for something suitable for Joseph to wear. I just ended up picking a black robe to help him blend in better.

And then it was time for payment. Removing the backpack from my shoulders, I reached inside and pulled out the smallest coin that I could find. Even still, the clothes we were buying would be worth only a tiny fraction of it.

The woman frowned as I placed the coin on the table. Then looked back at me.

"Hm? I only accept cash," she replied in Arabic.

"This is all I have," I replied, also in Arabic.

She picked it up and stared at it. I guessed she thought it was fake. I couldn't blame her. What moron would pay for a few garments with a gold coin of this weight? She placed it between her teeth and bit hard. I was about to walk away with the clothes, but she said, "No. Wait."

I heaved a sigh, even as I wrapped the new robe around me and placed the headscarf and veil over my head and face. She made her way over to a small vehicle where a man sat in the driver's seat—presumably her husband. I watched as she showed him the coin. He examined it carefully, just as she had done. And then he nodded.

She looked over at us. "Okay, you can take the clothes."

I scoffed. *Thanks.*

Joseph was still breathing heavily as we backed away. Once we were at a distance where he was comfortable taking a few steps back from me, he put on his own robe. Now that we were dressed, I resumed my position on his back and he continued running toward the borders of the city.

"Where do we head first?" I asked, as the sand gave way and we arrived at a concrete road.

"We need to find somewhere safe to stay until this evening."

I looked up and down the road, trying to see if I recognized anything about this area. I didn't. So Joseph just started running along the road toward where the most noise was coming from. We passed along narrow road after road until we eventually reached a square that was lined with shops. In one corner, I spotted a sign that read *Guest House*.

I pointed it out to Joseph and we arrived outside a mud-brick building a few seconds later. I climbed off Joseph's back and was about to head inside when Joseph pulled me back.

"Look," he said.

He pointed to a poster attached to one of the lamp posts. A poster with my, Lalia's, and Hassan's passport photos on it. I guessed this was one of many posters that were put up the night I disappeared too.

"Oh."

"It's a good thing you're wearing a niqab," Joseph said quietly. "You don't want to be seen by anyone now that the hunters are after you... Let's keep moving."

I tore my eyes away from the poster as Joseph ushered me into the building. We found ourselves in a small bare-walled reception room that reeked of detergent. There was a desk in the center of it, but nobody was sitting behind it. I rang the brass bell four times.

A man with a unibrow and a thick bushy mustache emerged from one of the back rooms.

Joseph's grip around my waist was almost painful.

"Yes?" the man said in English, looking from me to Joseph.

"We would like a room," I replied in Arabic as I

clutched Joseph's hands around my waist and loosened them slightly. "Just until this evening."

He eyed Joseph more closely. "Are you married?"

"No," I replied, already realizing where this was heading.

"We don't allow cohabiting between unmarried men and women. You will need to book separate—"

"We won't be sleeping here. We'll be leaving tonight, as I said."

He looked at me suspiciously. "You are not Egyptian nationals? I will need to see your passports."

"We don't have passports with us."

"Then I'm sorry, we can't accommodate you here."

I breathed out in frustration. Sliding the backpack off my back, I pulled out another gold coin and planted it on the desk none too gently.

"How about now?"

His eyes widened as he looked down at the coin. He picked it up and examined it. He was faster to realize its value than the clothes merchant. He nodded toward a narrow staircase.

"All right," he said. Reaching into one of the

drawers, he pulled out a key and handed it to me. "Until this evening only?"

That coin might have paid for a hundred nights in this basic guesthouse.

I just nodded politely. "Please, and I hope you'll provide drinking water."

"Of course," he said, bowing his head.

He walked back through the door he'd first entered from and returned a moment later with a two-liter bottle of water. He handed it to me, and then Joseph and I made our way up the staircase.

"You seem to be getting a bit better around humans?" I asked, once we were out of earshot.

"Only because I'm practically smothering you," he said. "Even with you standing a foot away, I can feel the difference."

We found our room—small, with twin beds lining opposite walls. It was very basic, but it seemed clean. We locked ourselves inside. After opening the bottle of water and chugging down an entire liter, I offered the bottle to Ben. He declined.

I tore off my niqab and then hurried over to one of

the twin beds. I grabbed the blanket, wrapping it around me. It was too thin to provide me much warmth. I was grateful when Joseph reached for the blanket on his own bed, walked over and wrapped that around my shoulders too.

"Thanks," I said.

He sat down on the bed opposite me and breathed out slowly, rubbing his face with his hands. Then he looked up and stared at me.

"River... there's something I should probably tell you about myself."

I raised a brow. "What?"

"My name is not Joseph Brunson."

I stared at him. "Huh?"

"My name is Benjamin Novak. Or Ben, if you like."

"Ben-Benjamin Novak... Why would you want to keep your name a secret?"

He leaned back on the bed. "That's kind of a long story. But I'm prince of an island known as The Shade. It's an island unknown to mainstream society. My parents rule the place, and it's a haven for all vampires and other supernaturals."

My mind was reeling.

Joseph—Ben—is a prince?

The Shade?

"Then… if that's your home, how on earth did you end up trapped in The Oasis?"

"I left The Shade after my father turned me into a vampire, because I displayed… unusual symptoms. Symptoms that nobody else on the island had displayed in such severity. And I did something bad. Very bad."

"What?"

"I murdered one of my own people."

Wow.

"Most vampires are capable of drinking animal blood, however disgusting it is for them. But I was physically incapable of it. I couldn't risk killing another person, and in my position, leaving was the only right thing to do. I swore that I wouldn't return until I'd figured out what was wrong with me."

"But, Ben," I said, frowning, "you told me before that you know how to cure vampirism. Why don't you just take that cure and turn back into a human?"

He paused before answering. "There was a reason

my father turned me into a vampire. My birth… let's just say that it was unusual. My blood as a human was deemed valuable by enemies of my parents and made me a target, and so I turned. But even if that threat had passed by now, I'm not sure I could live the rest of my life as a human. Almost everyone I care about—my whole family, except for my sister, and most of my friends—are vampires. I always expected to turn into one as soon as my parents agreed. Growing old and dying while everyone in my life lives on… " His voice trailed off.

"How old is your sister?"

"She's my twin," he replied. "We're both…" He stopped. "I think our birthday was just recently. I've lost track of the date. But I think we're eighteen by now—although I turned when I was seventeen."

I was surprised. He seemed older than seventeen.

"I'm seventeen, too," I said.

I became quiet as I tried to process all that he'd just told me. Then he dropped another brick on me.

"There's also something else I should tell you, River… as a half blood, you won't age."

"What?"

"You're immortal. Just like vampires. You never age past the age when you were turned. You won't pass away from this world unless someone manages to kill you."

"Immortal," I gasped. I couldn't wrap my mind around the word.

It was still too much to take in at once. I felt overwhelmed. The implications of such a notion began to flood my brain.

"But… But my family. They are not immortal."

Ben shook his head.

"I-I can't be immortal. I can't remain while everyone I love dies around me." *Just like you can't die while everyone you love lives.*

Ben lowered his eyes to the floor, his face ashen.

"How come you didn't mention this before?"

"I couldn't find the right opportunity," he said.

"There must be a way for me to turn back into a human!" I stood up, the blankets falling to my feet. I looked at Ben in desperation. "There must be some way to cure me."

He looked doubtful. "It's possible that there is a cure. But as I mentioned before, it won't be easy to find, and I have no idea what it might be." He paused, wetting his lower lip. "But… I do know some people who might be able to help you. Back in The Shade. There are people there more knowledgeable and experienced than me. I'm not sure how to reach there from here, and I wouldn't set foot with you on the island—"

"Why not?"

"I still have my own mysteries to solve… But I can try to help you get there."

"You'd do that for me?"

He shrugged. "I can't just leave you stranded like this."

I fell silent, still trying to process everything he had just told me. *Immortal. I'm immortal.* That was insane.

The idea of never dying—never growing past seventeen—was terrifying to me.

But Ben's words had provided at least some thread of comfort that perhaps there was hope for me. That we might discover a way for me to turn back into a human and return to my family who so desperately needed me.

I fixed my eyes on Ben's stoic face. And once again I caught myself wondering why he would put himself out for me like this. I wasn't used to this sort of kindness without some expectation in return.

I drifted off into my own thoughts, and, it seemed, so did he. We were silent for a long time, until finally I asked the question that had been at the back of my mind ever since we left The Oasis.

"Ben. Why do you think Jeramiah let us go so easily?"

His eyes darkened.

"I'm not sure why. But I hope we never find out."

Epilogue: Derek

I looked around our long candle-lit table. We'd pulled it out onto the veranda to dine beneath the stars. Surrounding me were some of my closest friends and family. Sofia sat next to me on my right, Rose on my left, while Caleb sat on the other side of my daughter. Further along the table were Eli, Vivienne and Xavier; Kiev and Mona; Aiden and Kailyn; Gavin, Zinnia and Griffin; Ashley and Landis; Anna and Kyle; Corrine and Ibrahim; and, of course, the two guests of honor—Yuri and Claudia. The latter had just returned from their belated honeymoon to Paris and had successfully accomplished what they'd set out to do. Claudia was now officially pregnant.

She positively beamed as she sat at the opposite end of the table, digging into the meal Sofia and I had prepared together. They had not been gone long—not that any of us had expected it to take long.

Claudia's animated voice filled my ears as I ate from my own plate of food, while all the vampires present just drank blood. Claudia dominated the conversation, asking question after question about what had happened on the island since they'd been gone.

"You missed Caleb's and my wedding," Rose said, through a mouthful of quiche. She held up her ring finger.

"Oh, my God. You got married!" Claudia practically bounced in her chair. "Are you going to turn into a vampire?"

Rose shot me a sideways glance, wiping her mouth with a napkin. "We don't know yet," she replied. "Ben still hasn't returned and we still don't know what went wrong with his turning... So we're just waiting for now."

"What about your honeymoon?" Claudia asked.

Rose blushed as she looked at her new husband. "We're still deciding on that also…"

Sofia changed the subject and proceeded to explain about the dragons. Claudia seemed to be most interested in gossip about the relationships the fire-breathers had struck up with the humans around the island. Not that it interested me much. Rose mentioned that none of the girls had revealed any details about their relationships, but they all seemed to be exceptionally happy—which was all that mattered.

As for the dragon prince, he had left unexpectedly after my daughter's wedding, and nobody was sure exactly where he'd gone, or if he would ever be returning.

"You're going to have to do some detective work yourself about those dragons, Claudia," Vivienne said, grinning. "Those girls are tight-lipped."

I smiled at my sister, eyeing her growing bump. She grew more luminous by the day. We still didn't know if she was carrying a boy or a girl, but none of us could wait to meet our newest addition to the family.

By the end of the meal, we'd recounted everything else that had happened that we could think of while Claudia and Yuri had been in Paris. After a dessert of cheesecake and fresh fruit, I leaned back in my chair, listening to the conversations around me. Then I locked eyes with Xavier. I nodded subtly, and he nodded back.

I leaned over to Sofia, who was chatting with Corrine, and kissed her neck.

"I'll see you later," I said softly.

My wife understood where I was going. She squeezed my hand and kissed me back.

Then I took my leave with Xavier. We headed out of the penthouse and made our way down to the ground. We walked silently through the forest and to the Port. A seventeen-foot boat was waiting at the end of the jetty—a new one that Caleb had recently designed. Xavier and I boarded it and navigated it across the waves toward the boundary of the island. We stopped just before we reached it and scanned the ocean surrounding us.

Even without vampire vision, I could see clearly three large gray ships floating in the distance.

"So they're still here," I muttered.

"They're too close to The Shade for this to be a coincidence," Xavier said.

Of course, he was right. These ships had first been spotted by Micah three days ago, and they had been floating in the same area ever since. Clearly, they were also strategically distanced from each other—the space between the three of them was identical. Their presence here was precise and calculated.

Someone had discovered The Shade's location, and was watching us.

And that someone was a hunter.

There had been several more sightings of supernatural creatures in the past week that had been picked up by mainstream media—sightings that had not been of anyone from The Shade. No, there were other supernaturals who knew how to enter the human realm, and they were no longer bothering to keep themselves hidden since the code of secrecy had been broken.

The most recent sighting had been a trio of ogres, up in Canada, near Mount Logan. The most disconcerting thing was that Mona's map marked many gates connecting this human realm to the supernatural one. But there wasn't a gate within hundreds of miles of Mount Logan. And there was no way that three huge ogres could've traveled that far without being noticed. This left us with the chilling conclusion that there were more entrances into the human realm than were marked on the map. Which meant that, even if we managed to close every single gate listed on this map, there were still other ways supernaturals were getting into this human realm.

I looked from one gray ship to the other. They looked like naval ships.

Eli and Aiden were convinced that the hunters were no longer the clandestine organization they had once been—funded by independent backers with a personal grudge against bloodsuckers. Rather, Eli and my father-in-law believed that the hunters were now being supported directly by the government. All of this exposure in mainstream media was striking panic in people and putting enormous pressure on leaders to take drastic action.

That meant that these hunters would soon be—or perhaps already were—a very different breed than any we'd experienced before. Being backed by the government meant they had unprecedented resources, and they were no longer just driven by a blind thirst for revenge. I could foresee a future where becoming a hunter would be a career route for young people, much like joining the Navy. The new generation of hunters would be cool, calculated, more technologically advanced than I wanted to think about and driven solely by intelligence. And there would be many of them. Too many for comfort.

A strong gust of wind blew against me, making my skin prickle.

The world was changing.

And my son was still out there.

He needed to be careful. He'd soon find himself in a whole new world.

A world to which nobody knew the rules.

READY FOR THE NEXT PART OF
BEN & RIVER'S STORY?

A Shade of Vampire 18: A Trail of Echoes
is available to order now!
It releases September 25th 2015.

Please visit www.bellaforrest.net for details!

Also, if you'd like to stay up to date about Bella's
new releases, please visit: www.forrestbooks.com, enter
your email and you'll be the first to know.

a trail of echoes

A Shade of Vampire, Book 18

BELLA FORREST

23733564R00206

Made in the USA
San Bernardino, CA
29 August 2015